Spy Girl

Out
of the
Shadows

Carol Hedges

USBORNE

I'd like to thank my family for all their support.
Also the team at Usborne. You are the best!

First published in the UK in 2006 by Usborne Publishing Ltd., Usborne House, 83-85 Saffron Hill, London EC1N 8RT, England. www.usborne.com

The name Usborne and the devices ♀ ⊛ are Trade Marks of Usborne Publishing Ltd.

A CIP catalogue record for this book is available from the British Library.

JFMAMJ ASOND/06   ISBN 9780746070833   Printed in Great Britain.

A chess problem has unexpectedness, and a certain economy; it is essential that the moves should be surprising, and that every piece on the board should play its part.
G.H. Hardy, *A Mathematician's Apology*

Therefore keep watch, because you do not know the day or the hour.
Matthew 25.v.13

THE SHINY BIG MERCEDES SPED DOWN THE AVENUE DES CHAMPS ÉLYSÉES. IT TURNED INTO THE PLACE DE LA CONCORDE. THE SMALL BLACK ATV FOLLOWED IT, MAINTAINING A DISCREET THREE-CAR distance. Autumn sunlight danced on the river Seine as the two cars crossed over the Pont de la Concorde.

"He's heading for St-Germain-des-Près!" Field Agent Stash McGregor said excitedly. His partner Suki Smith gripped the wheel of the ATV. Her eyes narrowed as she focused on the road ahead.

The Mercedes began overtaking the cars streaming

along the Boulevard Saint Germain. Even by Parisian standards, this was totally unacceptable behaviour. Horns blasted, voices were raised and fists waved out of windows.

"Stay with him!" Stash exclaimed.

Suki edged the ATV out, weaving it skilfully through the traffic.

"Watch out – he's making a left turn!" Stash warned, as the Mercedes suddenly swerved off the busy main road, and into a quiet side street. Gritting her teeth, Suki spun the wheel and followed, trying to keep up with the much faster quarry.

At the edge of the pavement, an old man stood waiting. He wiped his coffee-stained moustache on the sleeve of his soft check shirt. Under his arm, he carried a wooden box of chess pieces. He was just about to cross over when the Mercedes shot into view.

The old guy stepped back, muttering angrily. The car sped by. For a few seconds, however, he had locked eyes with the man sitting in the back seat. He stared down the street at the receding car. The colour drained from his face, leaving it as grey as the locks of hair that straggled limply over his collar. Slowly, as if in a daze, he stepped off the kerb, just as the black ATV slammed round the corner. There was a cry, a squeal of brakes, followed by a dull thud. Then silence.

The Mercedes sped on towards the Luxembourg

quarter. The driver checked his rear-view mirror, then half-turned in his seat. He spoke in Russian to the rear passenger, "*On ot nas ushol, boss.*"

"Yes, we have lost them," the man agreed. His eyes glittered. "But it looks like we have just found someone else," he added softly. And he smiled, showing two rows of gleaming white teeth.

FOR MUCH OF HER LIFE, JAZMIN DAWSON'S PROFESSIONAL ASPIRATIONS WERE SIMPLE: SHE WANTED TO BE A SECRET AGENT AND A CRIME FIGHTER; SHE WANTED TO WEAR A SEXY OUTFIT AND carry a cool weapon. And right now, she had a further ambition: she wanted to be taller.

Jazmin stood in front of the bathroom mirror, brush in one hand, styling wax in the other. This had better work, she told herself grimly. She was so fed up with being teased because of her height. Or rather, her lack of it. She spent some time waxing and backcombing and pinning up her shoulder-length, curly brown hair. Then she surveyed herself in the mirror once more. Uh-huh. That was better. At least now she had tall hair.

Jazmin returned to her room, walking awkwardly as she tried to prevent her hair from obeying gravity and heading shoulder-wards. She really *really* hated being small. "Petite", her mum Assia called her. Yeah, right. That was the polite way of describing it. There were plenty of other ways. Jazmin knew many of them only too well, thanks to a certain gang of girls at her school who were experts in verbal knifeage, and who really needed to get a life and stop ruining other people's. Petite sucked. It was totally un-fun. She scrunched up her face in an expression of disgust. Her mum had no idea how the real world worked, she thought to herself sadly. In the real world, tall girls got to have their pick of everything. The vertically challenged merely got picked on.

Migrating to the kitchen, Jazmin helped herself to cereal while reading the note her mum had left propped up against the milk carton: *Working late – will bring pizza.* Her mum always brought pizza when she was working late. It was kind of a bribe, the subtext of which ran: "I got your favourite food, so in return, please don't moan at me." Jazmin sighed. Her mum had been working late quite a bit recently, and Jazmin was beginning to go off pizza.

Not that she was complaining, she reminded herself. She understood how important her mum's work was. And she was proud of her. Not many girls had a mother who was a Senior Field Agent for the ISA – the International Security Agency, a branch of the Global Intelligence Department. A mother who went on special assignments all over the world, some of which involved working undercover and carrying weaponry.

Jazmin drank some juice and tried to pretend to herself that she didn't have to go to the learning centre today.

She hated the learning centre. Nobody liked her there. The facilitators didn't like her, because she daydreamed her way through their lessons and never completed her homework assignments on time. The other girls didn't like her, because however hard she tried to blend (and to be truthful, she didn't try *that* hard) she was different. She wasn't a them-clone. At the learning centre, she was the outsider. An edge girl; she didn't fit in.

To put off the evil moment of her departure, Jazmin allowed herself to slide into her favourite daydream, which featured her imaginary alter-ego Jaz Dawson, secret agent and kick-ass gorgeous crime fighter. Eyes narrowing, she mentally checked out her well-stocked utility belt: gun, cartridge case, cuffs, pepper spray, taser and assorted knives (for medical emergencies only). Dressed in black lycra (with pink side-stripes), she visualized herself engaging in awesome martial arts stunts, while single handedly saving the world from evil and total annihilation.

Eventually, however, she could put off the moment no longer. Reluctantly dragging herself away from her gun-toting imaginary self and back into the real world, she got up from her chair and slowly went to locate her coat. Then she made her way to the ground floor.

Jazmin opened the door and stepped out. Straight into a large puddle. Eugh. She stared down at her shoes. They were soaked. How come she hadn't bothered to look out of the window and notice it was raining? She checked her watch. Unh – mental head slap! She was going to be late. And there was no time now to go back and change her footwear. And she had forgotten to bring her umbrella too.

Jazmin set off down the road at a brisk run. It was raining so hard that the drops were probably having to queue. Her perfectly styled hair was rapidly turning into a soggy bird's nest, and her feet were making little squelchy sounds with each step.

Oh boy, another perfect day in Paradise, she thought ruefully.

THE OLD MAN OPENED HIS EYES. HE WAS LYING ON HIS BACK, IN A BED. IT WAS NOT HIS OWN BED. AT THE FOOT OF THE BED, A YOUNG WOMAN IN A BLACK T-SHIRT WAS SITTING ON A BLUE PLASTIC chair. She wore a khaki combat vest and green cargo pants. Her blonde hair was tied back in a ponytail and she looked like she probably worked out in her spare time. He cut his eyes at her. The young woman was neat-featured, pretty. He grinned. "Zut! I must've died and gone to heaven," he joked.

The young woman raised her eyebrows. "I don't think so," she said, her lips curving into the ghost of a smile.

"No? So where am I then?"

"The British Hospital in Levallois, *Monsieur Brun*."

The old guy's eyes widened. "*Merde!* Who's paying?"

"We are."

He regarded her suspiciously. "Eh – we are?" he repeated.

"Uh-huh."

"How come?"

"We assume you don't have private health insurance."

"And 'we' would be...?"

"My partner and I." The young woman leaned forward, an expression of concern upon her face. "Do you remember what happened to you, *monsieur*?"

His eyes vague and unfocused, the old man trawled through his memory. "I was crossing the road," he said. "There was a big Mercedes and I...and then there was another car and..." He cut the young woman a sharp sideways glance. "You were driving the other car. You ran into me!" he said indignantly.

Suki bent her head in acknowledgement of the accusation. "I'm so sorry, *monsieur*," she said. "You stepped straight off the kerb without looking. Thank goodness you weren't really badly hurt. All you're suffering from is mild concussion and some bruising to your left side from where you fell in the road."

The old man lifted the crisp white sheets and peered down at his body. "Well, would you believe it?" he murmured wonderingly. "And there I was thinking..." He broke off, looked up at her, "And my chess pieces?"

"Are all here in your locker, quite safe," the young woman reassured him.

He sighed resignedly. There was a brief silence. Then he said, "Always the same, you youngsters. Why d'you drive so fast?"

"I don't usually," Suki said. "We just happened to be on a pursuit."

He glanced at her. "Cops?"

"In a way," Suki said obscurely.

"Who were you after?"

Suki didn't reply. He gave her a narrow-eyed look. "The Mercedes?" he said, and when Suki still failed to respond, he remarked quietly, "The man in the back, it was Nikolai Arkady, wasn't it?"

Suki stared at him in disbelief. "How do you know that?"

"I saw him."

Suki frowned, "I mean, how do you know Nikolai Arkady?"

He shrugged, eyeing her speculatively, as if working her out, deciding whether he could trust her or not.

Puzzled, Suki shook her head. "I don't understand. You're just a—"

"Stupid old Frenchman who can't manage to cross a road without getting knocked over," the old man finished her sentence for her. "Yes, right, I am *now*. And my name is Jean Brun, like it says on my ID card." He paused. Again his expression changed, becoming withdrawn and remote, as if he were going through some immense inner struggle. Suki sat still, silently watching him. Minutes passed. At length, he seemed to reach a decision. "But once upon a time, there was a then," he said quietly. "And *then*, my name was Ivan Kirilovitch, and I worked at the Arkadia Clinic with that man's father, Boris Arkady."

Suki's mouth dropped open; her eyes widened in shock. "But you can't be," she gasped. "I've seen the FSB report. Dr. Kirilovitch is dead. He died in a horrific car accident ten years ago!"

There was a long pause. Neither of them moved. The room fell so quiet you could hear the air-conditioning humming. So quiet you could almost hear their hearts beating.

Then the old man looked up at Suki, and his eyes were suddenly steady and glass-clear.

"Yes, well, maybe you shouldn't believe everything you read," he said quietly.

"DR. IVAN KIRILOVITCH!" EXCLAIMED THE HEAD OF THE LONDON BRANCH OF THE ISA. "AFTER ALL THIS TIME." HE GLANCED DOWN AT THE INFORMATION ON HIS DESK. "WE ARE SURE IT REALLY *IS* HIM, aren't we?"

Agent Assia Dawson nodded. "His statement checks out. Besides, he knows too much about the day-to-day working routines of the Arkadia Clinic to have made it up. And the hospital has run a DNA test on him, and his DNA matches that of Dr. Kirilovitch," she told him.

"Ivan Kirilovitch. Of all the people to run over, in all the capital cities of the world." The head of the ISA shook his head in disbelief. "What would you bet the odds are on that happening? A billion to one?"

"I've looked through the files again. They never actually reported finding a body," Assia observed. "The Russian authorities just automatically presumed that he had died in that burned-out car. There was no coroner's inquest."

Her boss eye-rolled. "Yes, that'd be right – useless lot! The FSB couldn't find their bums with both hands and a map!" he scoffed. "So Kirilovitch is still alive. Amazing! And we pick him up off a Paris street. Exactly as our people are investigating what Boris Arkady got up to at his clinic. Talk about a lucky break!"

"It certainly is extraordinarily lucky," Assia agreed.

"Do we know any details about what he's been doing all this time?"

Assia shook her head. "He's not saying much," she said.

The head of the ISA grinned delightedly. "Nevertheless. Ivan Kirilovitch! Quite a feather in our cap, eh? Great stuff. His testimony could be the breakthrough we need right now." He stabbed his index finger excitedly at the pile of documentation on his desk. "Kirilovitch was there – he was actually working at the clinic as a surgeon. Unless he was completely blind, he must have known what was going on. He must have seen something." He glanced across the desk at Assia. "You're looking worried, Agent Dawson. Do we have a problem?"

Assia nodded slowly. She sucked in air. "Possibly. As you know, under normal circumstances, we'd set up a small debriefing team in Paris and question Dr. Kirilovitch there on the spot. Only we can't do that, because it appears that he won't agree to it."

The head of the ISA leaned across the desk. "Why not?"

"Kirilovitch says Nikolai might possibly have recognized him. He isn't sure. They only saw each other for a few seconds. But he says that he'll only talk to us on one condition: that we relocate him somewhere else. Out of France, preferably. Suki says he's absolutely adamant about it. She thinks he's afraid Nikolai could come looking for him. Because of what happened in the past."

The head of the ISA nodded. "I understand." He glanced down at the report lying on his desk. "Kirilovitch has vital information; we can't afford for anything to happen to him." He paused for a moment, his brow furrowed in thought. Then he went on, "Right, this is how we're going to play it: we'll offer Kirilovitch witness protection and find somewhere safe where we can debrief him."

"I think that's a good plan," Assia agreed. "As a precaution, I've already asked Suki and Stash to keep a watch on him until he leaves hospital. Just in case."

The head of the ISA nodded. "Sound thinking. As soon as he's discharged, we'll find a place for him to stay. Any suggestions where he could go?"

Assia pursed her lips. "Well," she said slowly and thoughtfully, "it's tricky, I can see that." The head of the ISA watched her closely. Then suddenly her expression changed, her face brightened. "Actually, sir, now I come to think of it, I believe I know where we *could* put him."

The head of the ISA nodded. "Well done, Agent Dawson. I knew I could rely on you to come up with a satisfactory solution. I'll deal with the necessary paperwork and leave all the other details up to you." He shook his head in disbelief. "You know, I still can't get my head around it: the man is killed in a road accident in Russia, then resurfaces ten years later in Paris, living under a false name."

Assia nodded. "There's certainly a story there."

The head of the ISA shot her a swift glance. "Arkady and Kirilovitch," he said slowly. "What do you reckon? Something must've gone terribly wrong."

Assia nodded again. "I think there might well be a lot more to this than meets the eye," she said thoughtfully.

The head of the ISA raised his eyebrows. "Oh, I'm absolutely convinced that there's more," he said happily. "And I'm relying on you to find out exactly what it is."

SOME TIME LATER, IN A SNACK BAR ON THE OTHER SIDE OF TOWN, JAZMIN TOOK A BIG BITE OF HER CARAMEL-CHOC-CHUNK COOKIE AND TRIED TO THINK POSITIVE THOUGHTS. HEY, SHE TOLD HERSELF brightly, today had been A Good Day. She had learned lots of Interesting Stuff which, although she couldn't actually recall any of it right now would, at some time in the future, stand her in Good Stead and make her a Better Person.

And the reason she was currently sitting in Cookies-4-U all on her own was her choice, right, and definitely not because everybody that she knew had been invited over to Honi Delacy's house for a pampering session. Followed by takeout and a scary movie.

Jazmin broke a chunk off her second cookie (triple-nut-choc-chip). She was not going to get Hamlety about this, she thought. She reminded herself that she and Honi Delacy had never got on from day one. She repeated to herself that this was not her fault. So people thought she was weird: that was their problem. She reassured herself that most of the girls in her class were so shallow they made a puddle on the pavement look deep. And finally, she reasoned that if she was up for a bit of pampering, she could go home, play ambient music, light a few scented candles and run herself a nice, big, bubbly bath.

She had options. She did not need to be with other people to have fun.

Jazmin scarfed down the last bit of cookie and got up. After all, it wasn't even as if she'd ever been Miss Social Queen to begin with, she told herself firmly. As she had frequently been told over the years: she wore the wrong clothes, said the wrong things, was the wrong height and spent far too much time daydreaming, or with her nose stuck in a stupid book. Misconception followed her around like a dopey spaniel. But so what? Life moved on. Deal with it. She picked up her bag and headed out into the no-sun no-fun November afternoon. She had books to drop off at the public library on her way home. Places to go, things to do.

She set off determinedly across town.

The library, a big modern glass and steel building, was located on the ground floor of the shopping and leisure complex. Jazmin dumped her books on the counter and headed for the fiction area. According to Honi Delacy, the public library was the haunt of loners, überboffs and no-lifers. Hey, maybe that's why I always feel so right at home here, she thought, letting her bravado slip temporarily.

Jazmin selected a couple of the latest crime thrillers. Her favourite kind of fiction. She took them over to the issue point. Eventually, when she was old enough to set up her business as a secret agent and crime fighter, she thought to herself, fumbling for her card, she wouldn't need any training. She'd have learned it all already from books. She swiped her card and was just returning it to her purse, when someone behind her cleared their throat. Then tapped her lightly on the shoulder. Then said: "Er...hi there, how're you doing?"

Dropping her card on the floor, Jazmin spun round. There was a boy standing right behind her in the queue.

He was holding a couple of books and was smiling in a friendly fashion. Frowning, Jazmin stared at him. Then her face cleared. She recognized him. He was in some of her classes at the learning centre. "I'm good," she said.

"We go to the same learning centre," the boy went on, as if he'd read her mind. He placed his books next to hers on the counter, then bent down and retrieved her card from the floor. "I've been going there since the end of last term. My family moved to London from Bristol in June. You've just started at the centre recently, haven't you?"

For a fleeting moment, Jazmin considered explaining to the boy how actually, she'd been a student there for the last four and a half years, only she'd been away in Prague for a couple of months over the summer helping her mum on an assignment. Then she changed her mind. What was the point? Her life was complicated enough. If this boy thought she was new in town, fine. She might as well go along with it.

"I've seen you a couple of times hanging around on your own," the boy continued, swiping his card. "It's hard making friends in a new place, isn't it?" he said, looking at her sympathetically. Jazmin observed that he had very nice hazel-coloured eyes behind his titanium-framed glasses, and that even if he wasn't Mr. Totally-Lunchable, he was still quite good-looking in a Clark Kenty sort of way.

"Sorry, I don't know your name," the boy said. "It's...?"

"Jazmin. Jazmin Dawson."

"Right. Hi, Jazmin. And you've checked out some books as well." The boy peered over her shoulder. "Whoa – they look a bit fierce," he laughed.

Grimacing, Jazmin began stuffing the books into her bag. "They're for my mum," she improvised quickly, "she likes reading that sort of stuff. You know how they are."

The boy nodded. Squinting sideways, Jazmin read the titles of the books he had chosen: *A History of Mathematics* and *Introduction to Advanced Maths*. Oh boy.

"Wait up, I'll walk with you," the boy said, tucking his books under one arm. "Oh – sorry, my name's Zeb. Zeb Stone," he said, holding the door open politely for her.

Jazmin and Zeb walked together through the shopping arcade. Zeb, who was much taller than she was, strode on quickly, which meant that Jazmin, who was used to dawdling and window-shopping, was forced to take extra steps to keep up. "So Zeb," she puffed, remembering Rule One of the Successful Girl's Guide to Dateville (Ask Him Questions About Himself), "umm...you're like...into maths?"

The boy's eyes gleamed. "Oh definitely," he replied emphatically.

Jazmin cast about frantically for something clever and mathsy to say. Fortunately, Zeb didn't appear to notice her inability to come up with anything. "Recently, I've been looking into Zeno's paradoxes," he went on enthusiastically.

Jazmin felt bits of her brain suddenly going fluffy. "Yeah?"

"And Aristotle's refutations of course. It's incredible the way something dating right back to 1000BC can still be so relevant to us today, isn't it?"

"Mmm. Right."

"I mean, our whole understanding of the concept of infinity is based on these Greek guys and what they came up with. Amazing, isn't it!"

"Amazing."

They left the shopping complex and crossed the road together. Zeb went on talking happily about the neo-Pythagoreans and mean proportionals, and Jazmin went on pretending that she understood what he was saying and agreed with every word, while secretly wondering how anybody could be so incredibly boring. Even her teeth were falling asleep. Eventually, after a long, snooze-making, one-sided discussion about the distinction between number and magnitude, Zeb unexpectedly asked: "So how about you, Jazmin? Do you like maths?"

"Oh. Me? Err, yeah, it's okay."

"What sort of maths do you like?"

"I'm into calculating things, I guess," Jazmin bluffed, thinking back to her clothes shopping trip the previous weekend, and her futile attempt to stick to a budget.

"That's great," Zeb exclaimed enthusiastically. "Do you know, I've never met a girl who was interested in maths before? All the girls I know are only interested in clothes and shopping. Maybe we could work together? I've done quite a bit of vector analysis."

"Yeah? Wow. Impressive."

They walked on in silence for a bit. Then Zeb cleared his throat and said: "So...um, tell me all about you."

Jazmin did a face scrunch. She always found personal questions difficult to answer. Talking about herself didn't come naturally. Anyway, what was there to tell? She was fourteen and nine months. 1.57 metres tall. Could lose a little weight, but couldn't get it together. Curly shoulder-length brown hair. Blue-green eyes. A healthy disregard for authority. An unhealthy dependence upon cookies, chocolate and crime fiction. The jury was out on her social life. That was it, really. Briefly, Jazmin toyed with the idea of casually dropping in a few details from the exciting, fast-paced life of her crime-fighting alter-ego Jaz Dawson, just to make herself sound a bit more interesting, but decided on second thoughts to resist the temptation, so there followed a long and uncomfortable pause while she groped frantically for something to say, and Zeb waited patiently for her to say it. Finally, she took a deep breath and announced: "Uh – I can juggle."

Zeb raised his eyebrows and looked surprised. Clearly he'd expected something a little higher up the intellectual scale than circus skills. "Oh really? Err, that's unusual. How come?" he asked politely.

"Someone taught me," Jazmin said, then paused. Her eyes flicked away from Zeb.

Suddenly, to her horror, she felt her throat thicken, tears pooling in her eyes. She hadn't realized how much it hurt to think of Tonda Palach, the Czech student she had met over the summer. He had been her first real boyfriend, but the relationship had come to a dramatic and tragic end. The scars on her heart still hadn't healed. The pause continued, becoming more and more awkward. Then, to Jazmin's relief, they reached the apartment block where she lived. "Okay, this is me," she said, turning to face Zeb. "Thanks for the company."

"No problem. Hope your mum enjoys the books."

"What books? Oh yeah, right. I'm sure she will." Jazmin gave him a little finger wave. "See you around," she said, hurrying quickly up the front steps and into the building.

She got the lift to the third floor and let herself into the apartment. Dumping her bag in the hallway, she went to fix herself a snack. So, all things considered, it had been an interesting afternoon, she thought. She had a pile of good books to read, and she'd met a new boy, albeit a rather studious one. No relationships though, she told herself firmly. She'd already seen that movie, and she hated the ending. Though it all went to prove that you never knew who you were going to run into in a library.

In the kitchen, Jazmin hacked a loaf of bread into alarmingly uneven slices and slapped butter thickly onto them, while letting her mind continue to run on Zeb Stone. He was quite nice-looking, she decided, even if he was a bit geeky. And perhaps the maths fixation was just some nervous social thing. Maybe over time, he'd normalize out. She opened an overhead cupboard and rummaged inside for a jar of something suitably gooey to put on the bread.

Jazmin made herself a peanut-butter-and-chocolate-spread sandwich with marshmallow sprinkles, and carried it and her bag up to her room, where she arranged her homework book neatly on her desk. She always went through this little ritual every afternoon in the hope that one day it might inspire her to do some actual work. So far, it hadn't.

While she munched her sandwich, she checked her micro. There were no messages. No texts, no chat, no gossip, no scandal. Zip. Zilch. Nothing. Was she surprised? Not really. Jazmin pulled a face. A long, homeworkful evening stretched ahead of her. Time to initiate phase two, she thought. A candlelit, foam-filled bath. With suitably soothing music. And then to follow, perhaps some TV, while she waited for her mum and her pizza to arrive. And hey, she could always do her homework later, couldn't she?

She went to run the water for her bath.

NEXT MORNING WHEN JAZMIN EMERGED THROUGH THE STREET DOOR SHE WAS SURPRISED AND SLIGHTLY DISCONCERTED TO DISCOVER ZEB STONE, THE BOY SHE'D MET IN THE LIBRARY THE previous day, leaning against a wall, waiting for her. She stared blankly at him. "What are you doing here?" she blurted out rudely.

"Hi, Jazmin," Zeb said, grinning happily and ignoring the unfriendly greeting. "I was just passing by so I thought I'd wait and walk to school with you. If you don't mind."

"Umm," Jazmin grunted. Her heart sank. She was not a morning person, and it looked suspiciously like Zeb was.

"So tell me, how did you get on with your maths homework?" Zeb asked brightly as they set off.

Jazmin mumbled something incoherent. She didn't do intelligent conversation before 8.30 a.m. Also she didn't recall telling Zeb she had maths homework.

"Did you complete the page on quadratics?" Zeb continued.

"Unh."

"I thought it was fairly challenging when my class did it. How about you?"

"Mmm."

"What did you make of problem twelve?"

"Erm..."

"Yeah – that's just what I thought. I might have guessed it wouldn't fool you either."

Jazmin blinked. She hadn't a clue what he was on

about. She shrank into her coat and started to walk faster, overwhelmed by the sudden and very unusual urge to get to school as fast as possible.

Jazmin hurried down the road, trying to create distance between herself and Zeb. However, Zeb easily kept pace with her, even managing to walk and talk at the same time. He seemed not to notice the monosyllabic responses he was getting in reply. Reaching the learning centre in what was, for her, record time, Jazmin saw the usual group of girls hanging out at the entrance, exchanging news and spreading gossip. The group she didn't belong to. She gave them a cheery Hey-see-if-I-care wave as she swept past, and was immensely gratified to see Honi Delacy's eyes widen in total astonishment as she saw who was walking with her.

Jazmin glanced quickly up at Zeb as they went into the building together and smiled wryly. If only Honi Delacy knew the truth, she thought: brain like Einstein, conversational skills of a mollusc. They entered the foyer and swiped their registration cards. "Right," Jazmin said briskly to Zeb, "I need to go to my geography class now."

"Maybe we could get together later after school?" Zeb suggested. "We could do some studying."

Jazmin shook her head. "Sorry, uh – I have stuff to do after school."

Zeb's face fell, but Jazmin hardened her heart and resisted. She'd made a useful statement to Honi and her mates. Now she had her own life to get on with, and as far as she was concerned, it was a life that did not include hanging with a guy from Planet Pythagoras. "See you around," she said firmly, and walked off down the corridor without looking back.

THE OLD MAN HAD BEEN TAKEN BACK TO HIS TINY FLAT IN THE GRIM GRAFFITI-STREWN OUTSKIRTS OF PARIS TO PACK UP HIS FEW PERSONAL BELONGINGS. HE FELT NEITHER JOY NOR SORROW. He had lived in this small, sour-smelling apartment for the past seven years, but looked at it dispassionately: it had been more of an existence than a life. His real life died a long time ago, he thought to himself. Died in a wrecked car. Died in a cheap hotel room, and a long, cold, miserable journey to Arkhangelsk. Nowadays he just breathed, ate, slept and drifted through the routine of his days like a shadow.

"Can we help you at all?" the young woman called Suki Smith asked.

He shook his head. "I can manage, thanks," he said abruptly.

The young woman and her partner, Stash McGregor, exchanged a glance of sympathy and understanding over the top of his bent head. The old man knew instinctively what they were doing, but ignored them. He did not need their pity right now. He stood in the centre of the living room, deep in his own private thoughts.

The tiny flat was almost obscene in its poverty. There

was a bed, a single chair, a small wooden table, its top scorch-marked. A hanging cupboard and one gas ring made up the kitchen. A frayed carpet of no fixed pattern barely covered the unvarnished floorboards. Grimy curtains framed a rain-spattered window which looked out onto a concrete wasteland. An area under the window was damp-stained. The air smelled thin, as if all the goodness had been breathed out of it.

A dreary and colourless place, and at first glance there seemed to be nothing there apart from the few sticks of cheap furniture. But there was something. On the wall by the bed hung some tiny paintings. They glowed golden and crimson and deep blue, the rich colours illuminating the drabness. All the paintings depicted the same scene but in a slightly different way. In each one there was a young woman wearing a long blue robe and carrying a tiny child. The child stared out with clear, ageless eyes. In some paintings, he raised a hand in silent blessing. Light radiated in a circle from his head. The old man walked over and lifted the paintings down one by one. Slowly, reverently, he placed them on the bed.

"Know what these are?" he asked with his back to the two young people.

"They're icons, aren't they?" Stash said. "Religious paintings. I guess they're from Russia."

"Yes, you're right." The old man stared down at the tiny paintings. "Know how they worked, the icon

painters?" he asked them as he looked around to find
something to wrap the paintings in, then went on speaking
without waiting for an answer. "They used to fast and pray
for days. That was the only way they could paint an icon
as it should be painted. To paint Christ and His Blessed
Mother they had to prepare themselves. Had to be in the
correct state of mind. That's what they believed then, back
in the olden days."

The gold figures on the rough grey blanket glittered and
seemed to listen.

"They're very beautiful," Suki said gently. "I've seen
icons like these once in an art exhibition."

He snorted indignantly. "An art exhibition!" he scoffed.
"They didn't paint icons to be walked past on a wall. You
have to live with them, day in and day out, until you don't
even see them any more. That's how you get to understand
them. The more you don't notice them, the more you
realize what they are saying." He wrapped up the icons
carefully in the grey blanket. "These icons are hundreds of
years old," he boasted. "They belonged to my family," he
said. Paused. "They used to believe in all that religious
stuff," he muttered.

The two agents watched in silence while he stomped
around the tiny flat, collecting the bits and pieces of his life
and piling them on the bed. Finally, when he was satisfied
that he had got everything, he looked up at them. "What
about my Tolstoy?" he inquired.

Stash glanced round the room. He'd heard of Tolstoy; he was a classic Russian author. There were no books left anywhere that he could see. But the old man was staring at him anxiously. "No problem," Stash said airily, "we certainly wouldn't want to leave Tolstoy behind, would we?"

The old man cut him a sharp-eyed look. Then he drew aside a curtain to reveal a glass door leading to the fire escape. He unlocked it and made a low chirruping sound. There was a pause, followed by a scrabbling noise. A small black and white cat paced into the room, its back arched as it rubbed itself affectionately against the man's leg. He bent down to pick it up. The cat massaged under his stubbly chin with the top of its head and purred contentedly.

Stash closed his eyes and pulled a face. "Oh no. Please don't tell me this is Tolstoy?" he said pleadingly. The old man grinned at him over the cat's furry head. His ice-blue eyes glinted with amusement. His face wore the expression of one who knows he has conned someone into agreeing to something they probably shouldn't have. "You said 'no problem'," he remarked slyly. "Anyway, I can't leave him on his own, can I? It'd be cruel."

"He seems to have managed okay on his own while you've been in hospital," Stash said drily, while Suki extended a friendly finger for the cat to sniff.

"Ah well, cats can always survive for a couple of days

on their wits," the old man said. He set Tolstoy down and pointed to the bed. "Basket's under there," he told Suki briskly. "Cat food in the cupboard."

"I'm not really sure they'll be happy about this..." Stash began, then caught the man's sardonic smile. He shrugged resignedly and lapsed into compliant silence.

Yes, the old man thought grimly, as he watched his cat being placed in the basket, the food being bundled up with the rest of his belongings. *I bet they won't be too happy about it either. But they'll go along with it. Have to. Because you can't do it without me. At the end of the day, I'm all you lot've got, aren't I?*

He took a final look around. The only things that remained were the silence and the memories. He was happy to leave them. He followed Stash and Suki out, locked the door and gave the key to the concierge downstairs for safekeeping, telling her that he was going to spend some time in the country. He did not tell her which country.

The old man, his belongings and his cat were placed in the rear of Stash's black ATV. The cat immediately set up a mournful wail and refused to be placated. Stash and Suki got into the front and Stash drove the ATV swiftly away, heading towards the Gare du Nord.

As he watched the highrises and houses speed by, the old man allowed his thoughts to drift. He'd made a deal with these people, he reminded himself; this was part of the deal. Later, there would be other parts to the deal, although they did not know that yet. In a couple of hours, he would have to unpack his stuff, assume another identity. He shrugged, sighed resignedly. Thought to himself that actually, that was the easy bit. It was the unpacking of what he carried in his mind that filled him with dread.

The journey was over almost before he had made the necessary mental adjustment. One minute, they were pulling out of Paris, the next minute, the superspeed train was hurtling through the Kent countryside and they were in England. A second later, or so it seemed, they pulled into St. Pancras station. The cat finally stopped complaining, curled itself into a disgruntled black ball and fell asleep. He adjusted his watch. New place, new time. Everything was new. He sneaked another look at his new ID card which had been issued in his new name: Charles Smith. Hardly original, he thought, but it would do.

The young man and woman collected his stuff, helped him down, carried the cat basket out of the train. Then they walked him along the platform, one each side, as if he was a prisoner on his way to face the firing squad. *"The condemned man ate a hearty breakfast", isn't that what they always used to say?* he thought ruefully to himself as he stumbled to keep up with them. Only in his case, it was not true. All he had had today was a cup of coffee. He'd missed out on breakfast, and now it was nearly lunchtime.

"Soon be there," the young woman said.

"The car should be right at the end of the platform," the young man said.

He regarded them both without responding. He was finding their relentless cheerfulness rather wearying. He thought longingly of his silent but familiar flat, the friends he played chess with, the chestnut trees in the Jardin du Luxembourg, and sighed quietly.

Then he reminded himself why he was here, what he had agreed to do. He thought instead of the house in Ekaterinburg, of Anna and Natacha. He straightened up, squared his shoulders and stepped out proudly between his two "prisoner escorts". *Never give in*, he told himself, *not for a moment. Because that moment would be for ever.*

ASSIA DAWSON WAS WAITING IN THE RECEPTION AREA OF THE RETIREMENT COMMUNITY. SHE CHECKED THE TIME. NOT MUCH LONGER; THEY WOULD BE HERE SOON. ASSIA PURSED HER LIPS, looked around, trying to visualize things through the eyes of a complete stranger. She saw fresh flowers in a copper vase, she sniffed the smell of polish, observed a selection of daily newspapers on the low coffee table, noted that every surface looked clean and bright and shiny. It was the little details that made the difference, she thought. They did a good job here, and it clearly showed.

Outside, the lawns were neatly mown, the autumn leaves raked up. Windows sparkled in the pale sunlight. The company that maintained the properties and grounds really cared about the environment the elderly residents inhabited. That was the reason why she had fought tooth and nail to get her own father a living unit here, and why it had been her suggestion to temporarily house Dr. Kirilovitch here also. The more she'd thought about it, the more logical it seemed. If you want to hide a tree, you place it in a forest. Therefore, if you want to hide an old man, put him in a retirement community. And this was one of the best in London.

The old man would settle in here well, she thought. She'd briefed her father, and he had agreed to befriend the Russian doctor and help him get acclimatized to his new surroundings. It shouldn't take long to extract the information they needed, and then Ivan Kirilovitch could fade into the background once more. Assia gave a sigh of satisfaction: everything was ready and in place. She heard the sound of wheels upon gravel. A car pulling up. Two familiar voices. They had arrived. Picking up her clipboard, she rose and walked to the door, a smile of welcome on her face.

LATER THAT SAME AFTERNOON, JAZMIN WAS SITTING AT A DESK IN THE INTEGRATED RESOURCES CENTRE. SHE WAS STARING GLOOMILY DOWN AT THE SMALL SCREEN OF HER HANDHELD. AT THE TOP OF THE screen was the heading: "Why Meeting Deadlines Is Important". She pulled a face, flexed her fingers and typed: *Meeting deadlines is important* on the first line, under the title. She paused, stared into the middle distance and sighed. Being in detention was the greatest suckage alive, she reflected. And she got put in detention a lot. Being in detention squatted on her life like a toad.

Jazmin closed her eyes, took a couple of deep breaths. *I am so not in after-class detention,* she told herself. *I am lying on golden sand. I am by the blue ocean. I hear the waves, I am listening to the wind in the palm trees. I am completely relaxed, completely relaxed...* She opened her eyes, looked around and sighed again. Returning to the screen, she typed: *because,* then sat and stared out of the window for a while, waiting for more inspiration to arrive. She wondered what her alter-ego Jaz Dawson would do in these circumstances. Nothing, she decided gloomily. Ace crime fighters and super divas completed their assignments successfully. They didn't get put in detention. She was flying solo on this one.

Suddenly, a shadow fell across the screen. Startled, Jazmin looked up. Honi Delacy, in her kitteny-cute designer clothes, was standing by her desk. Well, surprise! Jazmin doubted Honi had ever entered the Integrated

Resources Centre in her life. She was sure Honi put the IRC in the same box as the library: a hangout for freaks, geeks and überboffs.

"Hey, how're you doing?" Jazmin said cautiously. Honi was known to bully people. On the whole, Jazmin preferred the people she bullied not to be her. Honi nodded condescendingly. "This is my friend Delta; she arrived last term while you were gone," she said, indicating the girl with her.

"Hi, Delta," Jazmin said automatically.

Delta smiled. The halogen ceiling light bounced off her braces, making them glint menacingly. The steel beads on her braids clinked as she swung her head forward. Uh-oh, Jazmin thought. A bitey girl.

"I've been looking for you," Honi continued.

"Peachy."

Honi grabbed a chair, scraping it loudly and deliberately along the woodblock floor. The effect was instantaneous. Heads shot up like gophers all over the study centre, and a chorus of angry "Shhh"s filled the air. Honi grinned, gave a couple of people the flick. She dropped into the chair and leaned forward until her face was a couple of inches away from Jazmin's. Jazmin stared at her in absorbed fascination. Honi Delacy used very white face powder. Her eyelashes were heavily mascaraed. The effect was curiously like two flies who'd crashed into a sugar bowl, Jazmin thought, trying to keep her lips from twitching.

"So, Jazmin," Honi breathed, twisting a strand of long white-blonde hair round her finger, and speaking in the slow, irritatingly patronizing tone of voice that she employed to speak to those pathetic souls who inhabited the twilight world of the boy-free zone, "here you are."

"Yup. Here I am."

Honi studied Jazmin, head on one side. "Funny thing, we were all kind of under the impression you'd moved away."

"Nope."

"So where were you last term? Helping out your mother on one of her 'secret assignments'?"

Jazmin winced. Honi was referring back to the time when they'd all started out at the learning centre together, aged eleven. Jazmin had made the big mistake of boasting to everybody about how important and special her mum's job was and how she often helped her out. She'd thought the other girls would be impressed and would all want to be her friend. Alas, as she quickly discovered, they weren't and didn't. Over the years, this big mistake had returned so many times to haunt her that she'd kind of lost count. Honi paused, still staring at Jazmin. Now a worried frown creased her alabaster-white forehead.

"What?" Jazmin asked.

"Umm – did you put on a little weight over the summer?" Honi inquired solicitously.

"No, I didn't," Jazmin replied indignantly.

"Uh-huh. Right. Sorry, my mistake." Honi smiled sweetly. She paused again, staring down at Jazmin's hand, which was hovering over the screen. Jazmin took the hint. She eye-rolled and rested her hands on the desk. "Okay, what's this all about?" she asked. "Only I do have some work to do."

"Yeah? Let's see." Honi leaned forward, stared at the flickering screen. She read what Jazmin had written, and sniggered. Jazmin cupped her hands protectively round her work.

Honi leaned in closer. "So, Jazmin, let's get down to business. I'd like a word."

"Really? How about oxymoron? That's always been one of my favourites."

Honi looked puzzled. She didn't do sarcasm. Then she waved a dismissive hand: "Like, whatever. I want a word about you and that new boy," she went on.

Jazmin frowned. "Yeah? Me and the new boy what?"

Honi pursed her shiny, lipglossed mouth. "I saw you both walking to school this morning."

"Uh-huh. Did you? So?"

"And I just thought you ought to know something. Didn't I, Delta?"

"Right," Delta nodded. Clank, clank.

"And the something I ought to know is?"

Honi's smile could have performed surgery. "There's no need to be so twitchy. I'm really doing you a big favour,

Jazmin, because I'd just so hate to see you get *hurt*."

"You're all heart, Honi. So what's the goss?"

Honi Delacy fluffed her fringe. "I don't think you should consider you and Zeb are an *item* or anything, just because he walked you to school," she said.

Uh-huh, Jazmin thought. Now I see where we're heading with this. I'm going to get the Big Warn-off. "Oh, I don't consider that we're an item at all," she said.

"That's good. Yeah. See, I think he probably feels *sorry* for you, you know. Because you haven't got any friends."

"Does he? Haven't I?"

Honi's smile had claws in it. "Well, I can't think of anybody *I* know who actually likes you," she purred sweetly. "Can you think of anybody, Delta?"

"Unh-unh." Delta clicked her teeth, swung her braids from side to side and smiled her metallic smile.

Jazmin reminded herself that the mark of a good crime fighter was the ability to remain totally cool, calm and in control in all circumstances. However provoked one was feeling, and however much one badly wanted to punch the person doing the provoking. "So, is that it?" she said icily. "Are you done? Gee thanks, Honi. It's really good of you to take the time to come and tell me this stuff. Now, I'd better let you get on, hadn't I?"

Honi Delacy looked as if there was quite a lot more she wanted to say, but Jazmin turned her head away. She stared down at her work, deliberately blanking her.

Honi watched her in silence for a bit. Then reluctantly, she got up, signalling to Delta that they were leaving. Both girls headed for the exit, making sure their high heels created as much noisy clatter as they could on the way.

Places to go, people to scare, fear and loathing to inspire, Jazmin thought to herself. She waited until she heard the swing door close upon Honi and her friend before she allowed herself to breathe a sigh of relief and raise her head from her work. A little of Honi Delacy went a long way, she reflected. Though maybe not far enough.

Reapplying herself to her work once more, Jazmin read what she'd written so far, then added: *deadlines are important and have to be met* after the word *because*. She paused, frowning. There was definitely something not quite right about that sentence, she thought, but she wasn't sure how to improve on it. She stared at the screen, while further inspiration went on failing to arrive. Honi's comments on her lack of friends had left her feeling like a two-week-old party balloon, and now her detention essay was clearly on the slide too, she thought. She might as well give up. She checked the time: she'd done her forty minutes' detention. Shutting down her handheld, she collected her bits and pieces together. When the going gets tough, the tough get eating. It was time to head for the cookie shop.

OUTSIDE THE LEARNING CENTRE, IN THE SHADOW OF A NEIGHBOURING LIME TREE, THE TWO BLACK-CLOTHED FIGURES STOOD MOTIONLESS, WAITING AND WATCHING. THEY HAD BEEN IN position since mid-afternoon. Students streamed out of the building, but the watchers did not move. They were there for one individual only. The rest were scenery. Finally, Jazmin Dawson emerged through the double doors, clutching her bag. A quick glance of recognition passed between the two silent watchers. They waited to see which way she went.

Then, as if at a given signal, they stepped forward together and walked quickly along the pavement after her. Their footsteps were perfectly synchronized, suggesting that they were professionals, and that this was a manoeuvre they had carried out many times in the past.

For a while, their target seemed not to notice she was being followed. She continued ambling along, a dreamy expression on her face. The watchers drew closer until they were walking one on each side of her. After which it was merely a matter of grabbing hold of her arms and holding them firmly, so that she could not get free.

THE OLD MAN WAS SITTING IN HIS BLUE-SATIN-COVERED ARMCHAIR, NURSING A COLD BEER AND CONTEMPLATING HIS NEW SURROUNDINGS. SO HERE HE WAS. IT WAS CERTAINLY VERY NICE. Very smart, warm, too, and dry. Very unlike his flat in the sixteenth *arrondissement.* They had done their best to make him feel at home, hanging his icons over the bed, placing his books and his few things on the shelves.

The English woman with the short mousy hair and air of quiet authority had given him a booklet about the complex, discussed shopping requirements, written down a contact number and arranged to see him soon for a chat. She had also given him a brand-new wristwatch, explaining that it contained a security tag and also a small defence spray. They knew that he felt anxious about Nikolai Arkady; they wanted him to trust them, to feel safe. It was important, she'd said. And she'd smiled. She had a nice smile, he thought at the time. Then they'd left him to settle in. Tolstoy, the cat, after making a thorough exploration of every nook and cranny, had scoffed down a bowl of food and curled up in front of the radiator. For the little animal, home was always where his bowl was.

Now the old man sat and sipped his cold beer. If only it was that easy, he mused, watching the cat sleeping peacefully. He marvelled at the little animal's ability to live its life solely in the present. Sometimes when he thought about his life, he felt a sense of detachment, like looking through other people's windows. Like dreams.

He suddenly remembered his first day at the Arkadia Clinic. He saw himself quite clearly, a man in his late thirties. He was standing in the reception area, feeling nervous and ill at ease in the new surroundings. He had smelled fresh flowers, and also something else, an unfamiliar smell that he did not recognize; his feet whispered in deep-pile blue carpet; he saw cream-painted walls hung with testimonials from grateful patients, many of whom were internationally famous media personalities or people holding high political office. (The reception area here at the retirement community must have brought the memory back, he thought.)

Then he saw once more the pretty receptionist behind the clinic desk. Her dark hair was pinned back in an elegant French pleat. Her eyes flicked curiously across at him while she talked busily on the phone. As she spoke, she alternated between studying him and her elegant rose-painted fingernails, until at last, she finished her call.

"Yes?" she said finally, slightly raising her eyebrows and staring boldly at him. She had probably priced his clothes, he thought to himself, noted his cheap, shabby suitcase; she knew he was not a rich prospective client.

"My name is Ivan Kirilovitch," he told her, then corrected himself: "Dr. Ivan Kirilovitch. From Moscow. I have an appointment with Dr. Boris Arkady."

"Ah, yes," she responded, slightly more respectfully. She pressed a button, spoke a few words quietly into the receiver, then looked up at him again.

"Dr. Arkady will be with you in a minute," she said, pronouncing his name in a tone of almost reverent awe. "He is with a client right now. Please take a seat and make yourself comfortable." And she waved him towards one of the two low cream leather chairs that were placed either side of a beautiful rosewood and smoked-glass coffee table. On the table there were glossy upmarket magazines, a heavy glass vase that contained a single white orchid and suddenly he recognized the unfamiliar smell he had smelled earlier: it was the smell of money.

As if watching the rerun of an old movie, the man saw his younger self sinking into the cool, soft leather. He recalled how long those next few minutes lasted. He remembered how he repeated his opening words over and over again in his head while he waited: "I really can't thank you enough for giving me this job, Doctor. It will be an honour to work with such a great and gifted man as you." And how in the end, when Dr. Boris Arkady strode into the reception area, his white coat spotless, his dark-grey eyes watchfully alive under the thick black brows, all he managed to do was stammer out a few banal and lacklustre syllables.

But somehow, it had all been all right, hadn't it? The famous doctor had smiled, clapped him on the shoulder, said something complimentary about "our promising new Moscow recruit", and he'd felt a huge wave of relief and gratitude flood over him. And then, the great man had led him to the reception desk, saying, "Now, Doctor, there's someone special over here I want you to meet," and the pretty receptionist had half-risen, blushing, as Dr. Arkady reached across the desk, took her hand, smiled and said:

"This is Anna, my beautiful daughter. Anna, I'd like you to meet our new, but *very* brilliant colleague: Dr. Ivan Kirilovitch. All the way from Moscow."

And he remembered, just as clearly as if it had happened only a few hours ago, how he had looked deep into her eyes and fallen instantly head-over-heels in love.

"OOOH, THAT WAS A MEAN TRICK!" JAZMIN EXCLAIMED. "YOU BOTH SCARED ME! I'VE GOT A GOOD MIND NOT TO SPEAK TO YOU."

STASH MCGREGOR REACHED OVER AND GAVE HER A HUG. "AW, you know you love us really!" he grinned. Suki Smith smiled and produced a small silver gift bag from her pocket. She held it out. "Here, we brought a present for you," she said.

Jazmin took the bag and opened it. Wrapped in a sheet of tissue paper was a china model of a two-storey town house. It had a tiny red-pantiled roof and was painted a soft ochre colour, exactly like the real houses that Jazmin had seen on her recent visit to Prague in the summer. "Wow – thanks, it's great," she said.

"Oh, so you're speaking to us now?" Stash teased.

Jazmin grinned. It was impossible to be angry with Stash and Suki for long: she was far too fond of them. "So what are you two doing in England?" she asked, putting her present into her bag.

"Walking you home from school," Stash replied innocently, falling into step with her.

"Don't go all avoidy on me. What's the real story?"

Suki slipped her arm through Jazmin's. "You've heard of witness protection, haven't you?" she asked.

"Sure. It's when someone who's seen a serious crime gets looked after until they can give their evidence."

Suki nodded at her. "That's why we're here," she said. "We've just accompanied somebody who's gone into the ISA witness protection programme."

"Oh yeah?" Jazmin said, in a "keep on talking" tone of voice. She looked at Suki hopefully.

"And," Suki added brightly, "of course, we simply couldn't leave without taking our favourite junior agent out for a slap-up meal, could we?"

"Certainly not," Stash added, taking Jazmin's other arm. "So, girlfriend, where do you fancy eating tonight? Dinner's on us."

Uh-huh. Jazmin understood. She had been told as much as they were going to tell her. So naturally, it was going to be up to her to find out the rest. "Well, I know a really good place," she announced, glancing slyly up at Stash, "only it's not cheap..."

Stash shrugged. "Whatever. Let's go."

"And," Jazmin went on, suddenly feeling extra-inspired, "I have this essay to do for school. Perhaps while we're on our way there you could help me out with it."

"Maybe. What's the essay about?" Suki asked.

Jazmin whipped out her handheld and flipped the lid up

with her thumb. "Deadlines," she said, looking at them both hopefully. "It's about deadlines. Why do you think it's important to meet them?"

LATER THAT EVENING, ASSIA WAS SITTING IN THE KITCHEN, NURSING A MUG OF BLACK TEA AND DRUMMING HER FINGERS IRRITABLY ON THE TABLE. SHE HAD JUST TAKEN A CALL FROM HER twin brother, Ian, a successful and affluent businessman. Assia pursed her lips, wondering yet again why one's best laid plans frequently went belly up without any warning.

Ian had phoned to tell her that he'd invited their father to visit him and his family for an extended period of time in the run-up to Christmas. "I think he's feeling a bit neglected, stuck in that retirement community all on his own," he'd said. There was a implied criticism in his words which Assia was refusing to take on board. She reminded herself that Ian had been generous in funding the move of their father into the retirement community and was always prepared to write out a cheque for medical bills or any little extras, but lived a long distance away in one of the new vertical communities just outside York. And he was a very busy man. She couldn't expect him to drop everything and visit their father regularly. Even though he clearly expected that she could.

Assia frowned, staring down into her mug. Ian was planning to drive over and pick up their father the next day. The trouble was, she'd counted on her dad being there to befriend Dr. Ivan Kirilovitch and keep him occupied during his brief stay. That was why she'd suggested putting the Russian doctor there in the first place. Damn, damn, damn, she thought. She had promised the old man that he would not be left on his own in a strange place. Left to wander off. Or to worry, and maybe change his mind about talking to them. The whole success of this operation, to close down the Arkadia Clinic and prosecute its owner for the horrendous crimes the clinic had committed on a vast, worldwide scale, depended upon keeping Kirilovitch happy and co-operative, so that he wouldn't wake up one morning and take off somewhere before they'd discovered what he knew.

Assia recalled that Stash and Suki were flying out of the country tonight. There was no possibility of them staying around to help entertain the old man. Her own department was run off its feet with work. She certainly intended to visit Kirilovitch on a daily basis, but that was primarily to question him about the past. Their relationship would be a formal one. She needed back-up, someone else to befriend him, but there was nobody she could trust.

Unless...

Assia Dawson thought about her daughter Jazmin. She admitted to herself that their relationship had changed a lot. For several years, life had been a rough voyage –

rather like sailing through a stormy sea, each day marked by the jagged rocks of blazing rows. Now, however, they both seemed to be travelling peacefully together through calmer waters, to pursue the nautical metaphor.

Maybe it was good they were getting on so well, Assia thought to herself, because it looked like she was going to need Jazmin's help on this assignment. She sighed. As a rule, she did not like bringing her daughter into direct contact with what she did at work. Events occasionally took unexpected and unpredictable turns. Safe situations became suddenly volatile. But right now, she had no choice; there was nobody else she could ask. Anyway, Assia reassured herself, at the end of the day, she was only tasking her with visiting an old man and keeping him company. Not exactly a dangerous enterprise.

Assia finished her tea and began to plan out the conversation she would have when Jazmin got in later. Then she placed her mug in the sink and went to power up her notebook. She had documents to read, initial reports to write. It was up to her to ensure that everything was done correctly. She owed it to Dr. Kirilovitch, to the rest of her team. One slip at her end and Assia knew that the Arkady lawyers would be on to it in a flash when the trial opened. There had to be no stuff-ups. Nothing must go wrong. Boris Arkady could not be allowed to escape. Not after what he had done. There was too much at stake, both professionally and personally.

THE PARIS CONCIERGE HAD DECIDED TO MAKE AN EARLY MORNING START. ARMED WITH A BLACK PLASTIC RUBBISH SACK AND HER HEAVY DUTY WORK GLOVES, SHE WAS PATROLLING THE OUTER AREA of the block of flats, collecting broken bottles, fast-food wrappers, leaves, deflated footballs, dog mess and the occasional syringe. She muttered crossly to herself as she located, retrieved and bagged each item of discarded detritus. They were pigs, the people around here. Filthy pigs. They didn't deserve to live in a nice house; a sty would suit them better, *les sales types*!

The concierge dumped her sack of rubbish in one of the communal bins. Then she made her way back round to the front of the building, where a big shiny car was now parked at the kerb. *Zut!* Now what? she thought. She stopped in her tracks and placing her hands on her ample hips, stared at the car, a sullen expression on her pudgy face. She went on staring woodenly while the passenger door opened and a man emerged.

The concierge transferred her gaze from the car to the man getting out of it. She studied him intently. Might be in his thirties, she thought. Maybe early forties. Difficult to tell. He had dark hair, brushed straight back from his forehead and neatly tied in a ponytail. Clean shaven. Her gaze wandered to his clothes. They looked expensive. Beautiful, light, camel-coloured overcoat, chocolate pinstripe suit, pristine white shirt, navy and gold tie. Handmade leather shoes. Nice. Very nice. Smiling, the man drew nearer to her and the concierge got a waft of his cologne. Mmm-hmm, this man didn't just dress rich, he *smelled* rich, she thought, her nostrils flaring.

The concierge allowed herself to unbend a little. She nodded coolly at the man and said: "*Bonjour, monsieur,*" keeping, however, a wary distance between them. After all, she reminded herself, she didn't know yet what he was doing in the neighbourhood. Nor what he wanted.

"*Bonjour, madame,*" the man smiled, showing two rows of perfectly even white teeth. He produced a leather wallet. "I wonder if you can help me," he went on, flipping open the wallet and taking something out of it. "I am looking for this man. Perhaps you have seen him?" he asked, and she thought she could detect some sort of a foreign accent in his voice. He held out the small i-pic, which the concierge could now see was the photograph of an elderly man. An elderly man with long, straggly, grey hair, bushy eyebrows and a moustache. The concierge stared down at it, deliberately making her face an expressionless blank. "Who's asking?" she said suspiciously.

"So you know who he is?"

"Didn't say that, did I?"

"But you have seen him around," the man persisted.

"Like I said, it all depends who wants him." The concierge squinted up at the man. "You from the police?" she demanded abruptly.

The man laughed, showing once again his perfect white teeth. "No, no. Please let me assure you, my *dear* madame, my interest in the gentleman is a purely personal matter," he said, leaning towards her and sending another waft of delicious cologne in her direction. "You see, I represent certain members of the gentleman's family who haven't heard from him for quite some time and are, naturally, anxious to find out how he's getting on."

"Ah," the concierge nodded wisely. She understood now. "Family quarrel, was it?"

The man smiled. "Something like that," he said. He winked at her confidingly. "You know how these old people are sometimes – temperamental, a bit unpredictable, huh? They lose their temper, say things in the heat of the moment that they probably live to regret. I have spent some time tracking him down, speaking to the friends he meets in town, and they directed me to this district. So, do you know where he lives?"

The concierge folded her meaty arms. "Maybe."

"And you'll tell me?"

"Yeah, all right, I can tell you. He lives over there in that building," the concierge gestured with her hand. "I'm the concierge," she announced proudly.

The man stared over her shoulder, his expression suddenly alive, his eyes lit with an inner spark. "Ah. So of course, you know everyone around here. And you'll also tell me his number?"

"Twenty-nine. But it won't do you any good, though. He's gone."

The man's face dropped. "Gone? When did he go?" he demanded.

"Three days ago," the concierge told him. "Young couple came round and helped him pack. Told me he was going to spend some time in the country. Didn't say when he'd be back. Took his smelly old cat too, thank goodness."

The man uttered an exclamation of frustration. He turned away. Suddenly, the concierge felt guilty. As if she was personally responsible for his wasted quest. As if it was her fault the stupid old fool had disappeared. Her cautious reluctance vanished away. Now she wanted to help him, this rich, beautifully smelling man. She wanted to tell him something useful. She racked her brains. And then she remembered something. "Eh! Monsieur!"

The man turned back, raised an enquiring eyebrow.

"Look, *monsieur*, I don't know if it's any help to you," the concierge said, "but I overheard the two young ones talking together while they was taking the old man's stuff to their car. Not that I was deliberately listening of course," she added hastily.

"Of course you weren't," the man agreed. He moved closer, his dark eyes glittering. "Yes? And?"

"Like I said, it might be nothing, but I remember thinking at the time, it was a bit strange."

"What was strange, my dear madame?" the man inquired softly, coaxingly.

"Well, of course I only heard a couple of words," the concierge told him. "But they weren't speaking French. They were talking in English. I don't know if that's any help at all."

The man paused. He seemed to be thinking very deeply. Finally, he nodded slowly at her: "Yes, madame. It is certainly very helpful. *Merci.*" Then, without another word he spun round on his elegant brogues and got into the back of the car. The concierge stood and watched as the sleek vehicle executed a rapid three-point turn, before speeding off in the direction of the city centre.

The concierge's eyes narrowed. Huh, she thought to herself. He could at least have given her a tip. Didn't look as if he was short of a euro or two. Funny how they were all the same, *les riches*. Short arms and deep pockets. And always in a tearing hurry. She stared down the empty street. Maybe she'd have done better to have kept her mouth shut, she thought reflectively. Then she shrugged. Hey, what harm had she done? She'd only repeated what she had seen and heard. And if, like the rich man said, it meant the old boy was going to be reunited with his family, well that had to be a good thing. Didn't it, eh?

THE OLD MAN WAS RESTING. HE SAT IN HIS ARMCHAIR, THE CAT CURLED INTO A FURRY BALL UPON HIS KNEES. FOLDING THE TARTAN BLANKET MORE CLOSELY AROUND HIMSELF, HE ALLOWED HIS MIND to drift away. On the table, the unfinished remains of his lunch – onion soup and herb croutons – grew cold and congealed in its blue china bowl. He had spent much of the morning telling his story to the English agent, Assia Dawson, the woman he'd met when he first arrived. She had recorded it all. Now he felt utterly exhausted, too tired even to finish his food. He often dreamed about the past; it surprised him how fatiguing it was to speak about it.

He had filled in some of his background for Assia. He told her of his time in med. school. His graduation, with honours. The first member of his family to become a doctor. Then he described his job in a Moscow hospital. The shock of life as a newly qualified doctor, at the beck and call of senior housemen, surgeons, consultants, nurses, patients, cleaners. Everyone. Then he described his rise up the medical ladder. The long, long hours he worked. How sometimes he was so tired that he would see sparks in front of his eyes, would have to stamp on his own foot to check he was still awake.

He told her about the time he sat in the dingy staff room reading the magazine article about Dr. Boris Arkady. How impressed he was with the work the doctor was doing in his clinic way out east in the Urals, miles from civilization.

The "miracle" cures he performed upon people, the rejuvenated and restored lives. He read about the groundbreaking treatments, the innovative research, and suddenly, he longed to escape from the drudgery of his own life. Longed to move out of the poky shared room in the grey block at the rear of the hospital, to the wide freedom of open spaces and new experiences.

He envisaged the snow, the fresh mountain air. He dreamed of waking to the sound of wind soughing through pine branches, rather than the noise of the hospital generator. He wanted to hear wolves howling in the forest. To see a sky so clear and pollution-free you could reach up and pluck stars out of it. (The Urals were freezing cold and virtually inaccessible for eight months of the year, of course, but somehow he conveniently forgot about that.)

He wanted his life to be different.

He talked about finding Arkady's advert in the medical journal for a doctor, three weeks later. How his heart leaped, how he felt that it must be fate, *kismet*. He knew, even as he filled out the application form, that the job would be his.

He recalled his younger self catching the Trans-Siberian out of Moscow that bright morning in spring. He stood at a carriage window, watching the sleek city high-rise offices, the white and gold palaces, the great green and red onion-domed churches rush by as the long train headed east. Headed back in time too, as it clattered through town after identical town, each with its bleak industrial strip, its smoking factories, its town square, many still containing a statue of Lenin, that old dead deceiver. So that eventually, he came to believe that he was entering an older, more disturbing world.

Now he closed his eyes, lulled into a feeling of tranquillity by the motion of the train in his head. He surrendered to the irresistible lure of sleep. Later, when he woke up, he would make himself a cup of strong black tea. Russian tea. Then he might sally forth and explore his new surroundings.

THE OLD MAN WOKE UP SUDDENLY. HiS HEART WAS BEATiNG WiLDLY, HiS THROAT FELT DRY AS A BONE. THERE WAS SOMEBODY iN THE ROOM. HE SENSED iT, RECOGNiZED THE FEELiNG OF FEAR. That heart-stopping bolt of electricity that roared through the body like hot lightning. He knew exactly what it was because he had felt it before. That time in the clinic when he was in Arkady's private office, in the dead shut-eyed hours of the night, and became suddenly aware that he was no longer alone. He remembered the sensation of filled space, the realization that there was somebody standing behind him in the darkness. And he remembered the voice. That familiar quiet voice, silky soft and chilling in the blackness: *"Ay! Ivan, now what are you doing here at this ungodly hour, I wonder?"*

And now it was happening all over again.

He sat very, very still, willing himself not to move, not to show that he was awake.

Then slowly, cautiously, he began to open his eyes.

"OH JEEZ, I'M *SO* SORRY," JAZMIN EXCLAIMED. "I HONESTLY DIDN'T MEAN TO SURPRISE YOU. ONLY," SHE ADDED, "I DID KNOCK. SEVERAL TIMES. AND THEN I TRIED THE DOOR, AND IT WAS unlocked, so I thought...uh, well, I guess I didn't think, did I?" she said, her words tailing off into uncomfortable silence.

The elderly man in the chair went on gazing at her in a dazed fashion. His face was practically the same colour as his hair. His eyes were wide, and he was breathing heavily through his open mouth. He looked terrible.

"Er...hey, why don't I go and make you a nice hot cup of tea?" Jazmin continued in bright desperation. "You've had a bit of a shock. You just sit still, I'm sure I can find everything." She sidled quickly into the kitchen. Unh, mental head slap, she thought. Poor old thing, she only meant to check he was okay, and she'd nearly given him a heart attack. How unprofessional! She could just imagine her mum's reaction if she had to confess she'd killed off her chief witness. She didn't think the ISA would be too pleased either.

Jazmin plugged in the kettle. Strong tea, she told herself.

That's what he needed now. With two big spoonfuls of sugar to help him get over the shock. Although, he wasn't the only one who'd had a bit of a shake-up, she thought. Seeing the hunched figure slumped in the chair, eyes closed and mouth ajar, she'd thought just for a moment that he was already...but thankfully, she'd been wrong.

BACK IN THE LIVING ROOM, THE OLD MAN TOOK A FEW MOMENTS TO REGAIN HIS COMPOSURE. THEN HE STOOD UP, STRETCHING HIS CRAMPED LIMBS. HE FOLDED UP THE TARTAN BLANKET, PLACING IT over the end of the chair. So this must be Assia Dawson's daughter. He remembered Assia telling him she might call round later after school. But seeing the small sturdy figure, with its mass of dark curly hair, standing there in the half-light of the afternoon, he'd thought just for a moment that she was...but of course, he'd been wrong.

"Here you are, drink this," Jazmin said cheerfully, re-entering the room. She handed him a mug of steaming tea. He looked down into its milky depths and sighed. They clearly didn't have the first idea how to make tea in this country, he thought sadly. He took polite sips, trying not to wince as the thick syrupy sweetness coated itself around the inside of his mouth. "A nice cup of tea, thank you," he lied.

Jazmin looked relieved. The old man stared at her, examined her. Now he could see her in a clear light, he realized that although she was not tall, she was much older than he'd first thought. A teenager, not a twelve-year-old. Her face was already taking on the structure of adulthood, losing the small child's soft innocent roundness. He studied her over the rim of his mug. He didn't meet many teenagers, he thought. Not one-to-one at any rate. Of course there were plenty of them on the estate where he had lived. They had mean, hostile faces, sneering expressions. They hung around in gangs in the stairwells, smoking and talking loudly, or else kicked their footballs out in the street. They wore cheap imitation designer clothing that their parents bought at the local Arab market. Teenagers. They mimicked the way he spoke, copied his jolting, awkward way of walking. He tried to avoid them, as far as possible.

He took another sip from his mug, then held it out to the girl. "Thanks, I'm feeling much better now," he grunted.

"Great," Jazmin enthused. She took the mug back to the tiny kitchen and ran it under the tap, thankful for something useful to do.

"So you must be...Jazmin," the old man said, coming into the kitchen to join her.

Jazmin shook water off the mug, inverted it, and placed it on the side to dry. She nodded. "That's right. My mum told you I'd call in?"

"She did."

Belatedly, Jazmin stuck out her hand. "Nice to meet you, Mr. Smith."

Who? He stared at her, frowning. For a moment, he panicked, didn't recognize his own name, felt bewildered. Then he remembered. "Ah, yes. Maybe you'd better call me..." He paused, thumbing through his mental pack of ID cards to pick the correct one. "...Charles," he said, shaking the proffered hand solemnly. "Yes. You can call me Charles, if you like." (After all, he thought, as the great English playwright William Shakespeare once wrote: *What's in a name?*)

JAZMIN WISHED SHE KNEW FAR MORE ABOUT THE OLD MAN'S BACKGROUND AND STORY THAN SHE DID. SHE KNEW THE ROUGH OUTLINES, BUT AS USUAL, HER MUM HAD NOT TOLD HER NEARLY enough. She never did. Of course, it was a great opportunity to hone her detecting skills, but right now she could use a few more guidelines. She did not know what to say to this rather fierce-looking, elderly stranger with his piercing blue eyes and thick grey eyebrows and funny accent. With her granddad and his friends it was different. There was always loads to talk to them about. They could chat for hours. Now she picked up a tea towel, ran it round the inside of the mug, then folded the tea towel neatly and placed it on the edge of the sink to dry. "Can I do anything else for you?" she asked him politely.

He shook his head. "Why don't you sit down and talk to me for a bit?" Leading the way back to the living room, he gestured towards a chair. "So, my first real visitor," he said. "Tell me all about yourself."

Jazmin sat and sighed. Ironically, this was exactly the question she badly wanted to ask him. She thought for a while, then feeling as if she was on some stupid quiz show, told him a few carefully selected details about herself. The sort of bland, boring things that gave away nothing and that she didn't mind getting back to her mother. She made a conscious effort to speak slowly as she wasn't sure how well her listener understood English yet. The old man paid careful attention, nodding his head in an absorbed way, although Jazmin couldn't help suspecting that he didn't understand half of what she was saying and was only being polite about the other half.

"So there you are," she said finally, waving a dismissive hand. "Not that interesting, am I? How about you?"

There was a silence for a few minutes. Then he shrugged, and embarked upon a description of life in Paris, that quickly turned into the typical rant of seniors the world over. It was so stereotypical that at one point Jazmin shot him a quick look. Was he for real, she wondered, or was he also carefully crafting the sort of impression he wanted to make?

"Well," she said when he had finally ranted himself to a standstill, "gosh, you certainly know a lot about...um... the cost of things and...er...traffic, don't you!"

The old man looked pleased with her reaction.

"Do you have any other things you do?" Jazmin asked hopefully. When she'd agreed to visit him for her mum, she had kind of envisaged herself doing a bit of sleuthing, rather than comparing supermarket prices and bus fares, she thought.

"I play chess," he told her, adding, "I don't suppose you play, do you?"

Jazmin shook her head. "Sorry, no."

"Ah. Pity."

"I can juggle though," she added, remembering as she spoke that she'd mentioned this to Zeb Stone too. She wasn't quite sure why such a totally pointless skill seemed to have suddenly risen to the top of her attainment chart.

The old man's steely blue eyes lit up with sudden interest. "Oh? That's unusual. When did you learn?"

"Over the summer. I met some students from the Moscow Circus School. They taught me."

"Ah, the Moscow Circus," he murmured, a happy smile playing round his grey moustache.

Jazmin's eyes widened. "You've heard of it?"

"I've *been* to it. Many times. When I was a young man. It's on the Vernadskovo Prospect Seven. Near Sparrow Hills. I don't suppose your mother told you I used to work in Moscow."

Jazmin sensed something useful opening up at last. She leaned forward, her face alight with interest. "No, she didn't tell me," she said. "Go on, please...tell me about the circus, and your work in Moscow."

The old man sat back in his chair. His eyes took on a faraway expression: "Well, what can I tell you? I remember the big top – blue and gold stripes, glowing in the sunlight, and sitting on a red padded bench high up at the back watching the trapeze artists swing across the air on thin silver ropes. And I remember..." He paused, frown lines wrinkling his brow. "Yes – that was it: there were brown bears. Four of them in yellow jackets, riding bicycles, and a troupe of bareback riders. And I seem to recall there were also tigers jumping through burning hoops." He sighed. "Magical times. Magical times."

Ewww, Jazmin thought silently. Gross. Bears on bikes? Tigers jumping through burning hoops? It certainly wasn't her idea of circus. It sounded cruel and barbaric. She didn't recall her friends ever mentioning performing animals. She'd definitely have had something to say about it if they had. She glanced at the old man. He had his eyes closed and seemed to have retreated deep into a world of his own. Or else he had dozed off again. "Well, it all sounds *very* interesting," she said pointedly and loudly. His eyes opened. He gave her a shrewdly penetrating look, as if he knew exactly what she was really thinking. Then he closed his eyes again.

Silence began filling the room.

Jazmin pulled a face. This was like cycling through treacle, she thought. "And your work?" she asked.

The old man shrugged. "It was just a job," he said wearily.

Unh, Jazmin thought. This was not going well. Seeking inspiration, she glanced round for some new topic of conversation, something fresh to break the awkwardness of the gathering silence. "Umm...so where is your cat?" she asked. "Mum told me you had one."

The old man shrugged his shoulders. "He's gone out, I guess. He doesn't generally hang around long unless he's hungry."

"You need to butter his paws."

"Excuse me?" He opened his eyes and stared at her.

"That's what you do to cats when you move to a new house. You butter their paws: it stops them from straying off," Jazmin told him.

"Ah. I see." He nodded solemnly. "Well. Thank you for telling me that," he said.

Another awkward silence descended.

Jazmin furtively checked her watch. Her investigation was clearly going nowhere. She'd been here twenty minutes. Long enough for a first visit, surely. She got up out of her chair. "Well, I'd better be on my way now," she said. "Homework to do. Worse luck. No, don't get up, I can see myself out."

THE OLD MAN GRUNTED. HE WATCHED FROM THE COMFORT OF HIS ARMCHAIR AS SHE WALKED TO THE DOOR, TURNING TO SAY GOODBYE. THEN SHE OPENED IT, AND DISAPPEARED OUT INTO THE late afternoon. So, that was Assia Dawson's teenage daughter, he thought. She seemed harmless enough.

He waited until he was sure the girl had gone. Then he sat very still for a while, his mind turning over old times, past memories. Eventually, he heaved himself to his feet and went to lock the front door against the emerging winter night. After doing that, he drifted into the kitchen to make himself a snack.

The cat was sitting outside on the window sill. As it came in, it opened its mouth in a silent miaow of reproach. The old man refilled the bowl. *"Priyatnovo appetita!"* he said solemnly as he watched the cat scoffing down its supper. "So, Tolstoy," he told it, "we've lived in some odd places in our time, but this one certainly beats all. They put cold milk in tea. How strange is that, eh? And apparently I'm supposed to butter your paws." He gave a short laugh, bending down stiffly to run his hand gently along the furry back. "Good thing we're not staying long," he muttered under his breath, "we might end up as crazy as they are!"

THE NEXT MORNING FOUND JAZMIN SITTING AT THE KITCHEN TABLE POURING MAPLE SYRUP ON HER BREAKFAST PANCAKES AND THINKING ABOUT THE OLD MAN. WAS HE A GOOD GUY OR A BAD GUY? It was impossible to tell. He seemed perfectly normal on the surface. But then, Jazmin reminded herself, some people were good at seeming. The detective inside her badly wanted to find out what lay behind the normality. The trick to finding out such things was to use her eyes and ears, she reminded herself. The other trick was to use her brain to connect them up.

Jazmin finished her breakfast and got ready to head out for another boring day spent learning pointless stuff. Sometimes she was convinced that attending the learning centre was stopping her from getting a real education. Opening the door to the street, she peered cautiously out and breathed a sigh of relief: super-geeky Zeb Stone was not there.

The twenty minutes spent walking to school every morning was her special time. It was time spent indulging in her favourite daydream – the one featuring Jaz Dawson, sassy crime fighter who thwarts the villain, gets the guy and has the perfect outfit for every occasion. It was time not willingly spent in the company of somebody suffering from chronic mathsiness.

Jazmin slowed her pace. She knew as soon as she arrived at the learning centre she was going to have to pass right under the noses of Honi Delacy and her henchgirls, who would be gathered outside waiting to see if Zeb was walking with her again. At least this morning she was not going to be glared at, she thought. Which was a plus point. Yesterday, the expression on Honi's face could have been strapped to a truck and used to clear snow.

To delay the actual moment of her arrival at the entrance gate, Jazmin decided to stop off at the mini-mart and top up her breakfast. (The way she figured it, if she had to breathe in rush-hour trafficked air, there was little point fussing about eating healthy food.) Arriving at the store, she selected a large slice of chocolate cake and a mango and berry smoothie from the chiller cabinet and went to join the queue waiting to pay.

At the front of the queue she noticed that there was a noisy crowd from her school clutching bottles of water and chocolate bars. Jazmin instantly recognized two of Honi's gang-girls: hair-clanky Delta and another girl called Fion. She quietly slotted herself behind a tall man in a business suit, hoping none of them had noticed her. She was going to opt for the "stay low and blend with the racking" option.

Carefully keeping her back turned to the aisle, Jazmin studied the goodies on display. Everything looked so yummily delish. By the time her turn came to pay, the cake and drink had been joined by an iced muesli bar, a small packet of nuts and a roll of toffees. Whoa, did she know how to shop. She handed over her goodies and paycard to the girl on the till, mentally promising that tomorrow, she'd look into doing some snack damage control.

Jazmin left the store, clutching her bag of munchies, and ran straight into the group of girls who were hanging around outside. Bummer. She was just trying to slink by unnoticed when Fion suddenly spotted her. Her face lit up. Jazmin's heart sank. Fion was a sharp-chinned girl with sly pale-blue eyes and a spiteful tongue. She and Jazmin had had several run-ins in the past.

Jazmin hastily tuned her facial expression to bored.

"Hi, Jazmin," Fion greeted her happily, "didn't see you *down* there." She eyed Jazmin's big bag of goodies. "Wow – are you working on a growth spurt?" she joked.

Jazmin cut Fion a smile so thin it could have modelled designer clothes. "Hey, Fion. Interesting top – are you wearing it for a bet?" she responded. Unjustified bravado, she thought, the story of her life.

Meanwhile, the rest of the group, sensing a fun time arriving, stopped what they were doing and began circling sharkily around. Fion stared hard at Jazmin, who could almost see her brain-cogs whirring as she contemplated her next move. Then Fion folded her arms and grinned. It was the sort of grin that hung around on sandbanks waiting for unwary swimmers. "On your own this morning, I see," she observed casually.

Jazmin made a great pretence of looking over both shoulders, then to either side. "Well, gosh, looks like I am. How clever of you to notice."

"No Zeb Stone today? Aw, shame."

"Yeah, tragicistan. But I can handle it."

"Of course you can – after all, you've had so much *practice* over the years, haven't you!"

The surrounding crowd sniggered appreciatively.

"Hey, maybe she got dumped," a girl's voice from the crowd suggested happily. It sounded to Jazmin suspiciously like Delta's voice.

Fion shook her head. "I don't think so. See – to get *dumped*, you have to be in a *relationship* in the first place."

Unbidden, a sudden vision of Jaz Dawson floated in front of Jazmin's eyes. She saw her numero uno crime fighter slowly pull out her five-shot .38 Smith & Wesson Chief's Special from its black, hand-tooled leather holster and aim it straight between Fion's eyes. Sadly, Fion seemed blissfully unaware of the danger stepping towards her. Jazmin's eyes narrowed. Her mouth set in a hard line.

"Aww," Fion scoffed, grinning delightedly, "did I hurt the little bitty girly's feelings? Naughty me. Smack on hand."

Jazmin knew that the sensible thing to do at this point would be to leave with her dignity intact. However, maintaining her dignity suddenly ran second to the pleasure of getting in Fion's face. "Hey, why don't you mind your own business?" she told her icily. "Better still, why don't you go and fetch some sticks, or bite a postman. Or whatever it is you do for fun."

There was a collective indrawing of breath.

"What did you just say?" Fion exclaimed, her eyes widening in disbelief.

"You heard me. Or are you deaf as well?" Jazmin added recklessly, rolling with the moment.

The crowd gave out a collective "Ooooh" as Jazmin turned and roughly shouldered her way through.

"Hey Jazmin Dawson, you come right back here!" Fion exclaimed.

Jazmin pretended not to hear.

"Don't you walk away from me!" Fion yelled.

Jazmin continued walking.

"You're going to get it now," Delta called out from somewhere in the midst of the crowd.

Jazmin kept looking straight ahead. "Yeah, yeah, yeah. Tell it to somebody who cares," she flung out.

Head held high and shoulders rigid, Jazmin power walked herself to the corner of the street. Then she ran. She didn't stop running until she reached the safety of the park, where she collapsed panting onto a bench. Her heart was pounding in her chest, her eyes and nose streaming. Jazmin bent over, sucking in air. Jeez, she was so chronically unfit. Good thing she wasn't escaping from some gang of criminals; she'd be easy to apprehend.

Resisting the temptation to look up, Jazmin stayed bent double until she felt she could breathe without seeing little black and red spots in front of her eyes. Then she straightened up and reviewed her situation. It was not good. People who thought nothing moved faster than the speed of light had never seen a rumour spreading round her learning centre. By mid-morning, everyone would know what she had said to Fion. And that she'd said it in front of a crowd of witnesses. Not that she'd actually used the *word*, Jazmin reminded herself, but that didn't matter. From now on, she was going to be as popular as a parent at a party.

Jazmin did a face-scrunch. It was going to take more than a magic wand and a few sprinkles of pixie dust to sort this mess out, she reflected. It looked like her mum's old Russian man was going to be seeing quite a lot of her from now on. Meanwhile, she always had her bag of goodies to keep her company. When the going gets tough, the tough get snacking.

Sometime later, feeling happier and very much fuller, Jazmin Dawson scrunched up the empty goodie bag into a ball, and drop-kicked it into the nearest bin. Then she picked up her bag and headed off towards the public library. She was not going to the learning centre today. She'd rather stick pins in her eyes. It was time for a little distance learning. The library was warm, it was girl-gang-free, and best of all, it was full of crime fiction. A good opportunity to indulge in a little career development.

THE OLD MAN HAD GOT HIS BREAKFAST READY: TWO PIECES OF TOAST AND A GLASS OF STRONG BLACK TEA WHICH HE SWEETENED WITH JAM, RUSSIAN-STYLE. IT ALWAYS REMINDED HIM OF HOME — not the tiny Paris apartment — his real home. Now he stood at the kitchen counter, staring out at the rain-soaked bushes. Last night he had been dreaming again.

The dream was a memory, the memory a dream.

In the dream, he was once more back in the Urals, driving his car through the forest. There was a suitcase on the passenger seat beside him. It was winter. The road had been cleared earlier in the day, and there were piles of snow on either side. The trees stood out dark and menacing against the pristine whiteness. He was driving very fast, but he was not unduly worried; he knew this road, every bend and loop. It was cold in the car because the heating had packed up again. He kept meaning to have the car serviced, but he was always so busy that somehow he never got round to it. To cheer himself up, he began singing a verse of the satirical drinking song he had so often heard bawled out in the local bars:

Ekaterinburg, that's the place that's best.
Winter twelve months of the year,
Summer all the rest.

Ahead of him, far below, he could see the lights of Ekaterinburg, glowing golden in the grey winter afternoon.

He launched into another verse:

Ekaterinburg, that's the place that's best
Work hard seven days a week,
Sleep for all the rest.

At this point in the dream, the car approached the big bend that swept round to the left and marked the beginning of the swift descent into the valley. Suddenly, he realized he was travelling too fast and applied the brake. Nothing happened. Puzzled, he pressed down sharply with his right foot. The pedal depressed all the way to the floor, but the car did not respond. His heart lurched. Somehow, his brakes had failed. And at a critically dangerous moment. He stamped frantically on the brake pedal as the car relentlessly accelerated into the sharp bend.

Now the dream went into terrifying slow motion. With a sense of cold detachment, he changed gears, counting them out loud to stop his mind from spinning into a black vortex of fear: "Fifth...fourth...third...second..." He turned the steering wheel, spinning it round until the back wheels locked. The car skidded across the road, mounted the far bank and toppled on its side into the deep ditch that lay just behind the snowbank.

The dream leaped forward. In this part, he was stumbling through the forest. It was night, no moon, no stars, pitch black everywhere. At his back, a sheet of orange fire was rising into the night. There was the hiss and crackle of flames. The hot, greasy smell of burning diesel. He carried his suitcase in one hand, a small torch in the other. He was using the torch to illumine the path in front of him. A light to lighten the darkness. And it was cold, so bitterly cold.

Next, he was walking, travelling on back roads because it felt safer, skulking in the undergrowth whenever he heard a car or a lorry approaching. Mostly, he travelled by night. As he moved, he heard rustling in the forest. Strange sounds. A distant howling. The wolves were running, he thought to himself, shivering. But which wolves? The ones who hunted animals, or the ones who were now hunting him?

Another segue. He was in a small room in a cheap hotel, neon-lit from outside. He took off his boots, and slowly removed his socks. Shocked, he stared down at his swollen, painfully frostbitten feet. Several of his toes on one foot were black and felt numb. He swallowed hard, gazing at them. He was a doctor, he had seen this condition countless times. It was called dry gangrene and he knew it was caused by prolonged frostbite. He also knew there was only one cure: amputation. That is, if he did not want to lose his entire foot, and maybe more, to bacterial infection or blood poisoning.

For a long time he sat motionless on the bed, staring into the middle distance. Then he went into action.

Hobbling over to the minibar, he opened the two small bottles of Stolichnaya vodka, pouring them both into a plastic tumbler. Half of the alcohol he'd use for sterilization, the rest he'd drink afterwards to numb the pain. After performing this task, he got his Swiss army knife and took it into the bathroom.

Back in the present once more, the old man cradled the glass of sweet tea between his hands. Soon, he would have to face another gruelling morning of questions. Recounting his story to the English woman. Lifting the lid upon all the things that he'd tried to bury in the past. Then it would be time for lunch and a nap. Then the girl would come round and ask him more questions. If he was lucky, he might get in a walk or a visit to the shop before it got dark.

So this was his life, the old man thought. He checked the time on the watch, reminding himself how the various security bits of it worked. He trusted he'd never need to use them. After all, they had said he would be safe here. He hoped they were right.

STRAIGHT AFTER LUNCH, ASSIA HAD REQUESTED A MEETING WITH HER BOSS, THE HEAD OF THE ISA. SHE NEEDED TO UPDATE HIM ON HER PROGRESS. SUCH AS IT WAS. ASSIA COULDN'T HELP FEELING that thus far, the old man was only letting her into carefully selected areas of his life. It was as if he was learning about her, testing her, seeing how far he could trust her. The trouble with this was that there were deadlines looming on the horizon. Reports to be collated and finalized. Time was not on her side.

"So," the head of the ISA said, sitting back in his chair and folding his arms behind his head, "how are things going with Ivan Kirilovitch?"

Assia nodded in what she hoped was a brisk and purposeful way. "Fine, sir," she said. "Yes, I think he's settling in okay."

"And he's giving you useful stuff?"

"He's beginning to. Slowly." Assia pulled a wry face, remembering the old man's folded arms, his stubborn words: *"Eventually I shall tell you what you want to know, Assia Dawson. But first, I shall tell you what I want you to know."* He was buying time, she thought. Spinning out his story. She was not sure why, but the delay had not been factored into her plan.

"I get the distinct impression that if I push him he'll clam up and we'll get nothing," she said. "I'm sorry it's all taking a bit longer than I had anticipated."

"So what have you learned so far?"

Assia smiled. "Today he told me all about falling in love!"

The head of the ISA raised his eyebrows quizzically. "Excuse me?"

"He described his relationship with Arkady's daughter,

Anna. How they first met, how in love they were. Then he
told me all about their wedding and their life together. He
even showed me a picture of his daughter, Natacha." Assia
paused. "I think it was a conversation he needed to have,"
she said thoughtfully. "I get the feeling he hasn't ever really
spoken about them since he left Russia."

"How old was his daughter when..."

"Twelve years old," Assia said. "Do we know what
happened to them?"

The head of the ISA shook his head. "Arkady told our
Russian team that some time after Kirilovitch's supposed
death there was a violent quarrel between Anna and her
father. She took the girl and left Ekaterinburg. Arkady
hasn't set eyes upon her since that day."

"And do we believe him?"

The head of the ISA shrugged. "Who knows, eh?
Whatever the real truth, she certainly isn't living locally
any more. Our Russian team has checked. So she could be
anywhere. Maybe she even remarried and is living a new
life under a different name."

Another lost person. Assia pursed her lips. The location
of Kirilovitch's wife and child was a further complicating
factor, she thought – although she reminded herself
that the "child" was now a young woman in her early
twenties. Nevertheless, so much of his life revolved around
the existence of these two figures that it was as if they
hovered unseen at each meeting. Pale ghosts from a

happier past. As if gradually, step by step, they were drawing him back into their shadow world. Despite her best intentions, Assia was finding it hard to stay detached and impartial.

"Do we have a problem here?" the head of the ISA asked sharply, and Assia realized that she had allowed her mind to drift.

"No, sir," she said firmly. "I'm sure I can sort it."

"Good," the head of the ISA nodded. "Do what you can to speed things up, Agent Dawson. I gather they're hoping to hold the preliminary trial hearings straight after Christmas. Kirilovitch must know something about what was really going on. We need his testimony pretty soon."

Assia was in a subdued mood as she caught the train back home. She thought of the old man, so far from his native land, and his very-much-beloved wife and daughter whom he had left behind such a long time ago. There had to be justice done here, she thought grimly. The case against Boris Arkady had to succeed. And whatever it took, she had a duty of care for Kirilovitch while he remained under the ISA's protection.

Assia got off the train and walked the couple of streets to her apartment. She entered the downstairs lobby and carried her briefcase and notebook up the three flights of stairs (so much better for her legs than getting the lift).

At the top of the stairs, she paused, fumbling in her

shoulder bag for her bunch of keys. That was when she first noticed the figure in the shadows. He was leaning casually against the wall. Waiting. Assia slowly withdrew the keys from her bag, slotting them quickly and unobtrusively between her fingers in case she had to defend herself. Then, head erect and looking straight ahead, she walked confidently to her front door. The figure saw her coming, and detached itself from the shadows. It moved swiftly and silently towards her.

JAZMIN GLARED AT THE LIBRARY'S COMPUTER SCREEN AND UTTERED AN EXCLAMATION OF ANNOYANCE. HOW HAD SHE EVER THOUGHT CHESS WAS JUST A SIMPLE OLD BOARD GAME? HOW stupid was she?! She made her next move. There was a pause. Then the library's cyber-chess tutor informed her that her pawns could only move forward one square at a time and would she like to reconsider? Jazmin angrily typed in *No*. There was another pause. Her invisible cyber instructor moved one of its pieces and informed her smugly that once again she was in check. Jazmin swore at it.

A couple of kids, who were hanging about the games area, wandered across and stared at the screen. One of them, a solemn small boy who looked to be about six years old, advised her that she could mount an effective defence by moving her rook and bishop to block her opponent's piece. Jazmin asked him which one was the rook again, whereupon the boy gave her a long hard stare and went away.

Ewww. How embarrassing, she thought.

Jazmin had been on the Absolute Beginners Programme all afternoon, but she had forgotten how most of the pieces moved and was losing every game. There had to be an easier way to learn this stupid thing, she thought grimly. Okay, she really wanted to help the old man feel at home, but not at the expense of her personal sanity. Right now, she was beginning to see black and white squares in front of her eyes even when she wasn't looking at the screen. And all the references to pawns was making her think of prawns and reminding her that she was a long way from food. Maybe it was time to quit. Home and a full fridge were summoning her.

Letting herself back into the apartment, Jazmin was surprised to hear the sound of voices coming from the kitchen. Her mum must have a visitor, she thought. Funny, she didn't remember being told to expect anybody. Sounded like a male visitor too, but not the old man. She set her bag down quietly and tiptoed to the half-closed door. She applied an ear cautiously to the crack and listened, her eyes slowly widening and the expression on her face altering from curiosity to total disbelief.

JAZMIN WAVED GOODBYE TO THE VISITOR, AND CLOSED THE LOBBY DOOR. THEN SHE LEANED HER HEAD AGAINST THE DOOR AND GROANED LOUDLY. THANKS, ZEB, SHE THOUGHT SARCASTICALLY. Thank you *sooo* much. It was really kind of you to call round with the homework I missed today. It was especially kind of you to hang around the hallway, introduce yourself to my mum and get invited in for a drink when you could've just posted the stuff through the letterbox.

Unh! Jazmin banged her forehead against the door a couple of times. Sheesh! Sometimes she felt just like a hedgehog in the Fast Lane of Life, she thought. Jazmin knew her mother turned a blind eye to quite a lot of things, but skipping school featured right at the top of her Don't-do List. She was going to be majorly mad. On the maternal freak-o-meter, she was probably already at an eight and rising. Sighing resignedly, she dragged her reluctant feet back to the apartment. It was time to face the music.

Jazmin headed towards the kitchen, where she discovered her mum getting dinner ready. She decided to lurk in the doorway just in case she needed to make a speedy exit up to her room in the next few minutes. Her mum went on placidly chopping veggies. She was using the big, sharp Sabatier knife, Jazmin observed from the safety of the doorway. She hoped it was not symbolic of anything.

"Nice boy," Assia remarked, looking up from the chopping board.

Jazmin shrugged. "He's okay, I suppose. Bit geeky."

"You know, I never realized that you were that keen on studying."

"Yeah – heh, heh, life's full of surprises, isn't it!"

Assia carefully set down the knife on the chopping board. Then she turned, folded her arms and regarded her daughter thoughtfully. "So..." she said slowly. And waited.

Jazmin had certain fixed principles. She only lied at such times when the truth didn't seem appropriate. This was one of those times. "Yeah, wow – I can't understand how I forgot to collect that homework," she exclaimed, innocence hanging from her words like loops of toffee.

Assia raised her eyebrows. "No?"

Jazmin expelled air, shaking her head. "Riddichio," she said. "And how did I manage to miss Zeb? I must have been daydreaming. Duh!" She flashed her mum a winning smile. "Well, guess I'd better hit the books then, hadn't I?" she said cheerfully. She cut her eyes towards the hob. "Ooh – is that cauliflower cheese? Yum – my favourite. Give me a shout when it's ready, won't you?"

Jazmin scooted out of the kitchen, breathing a sigh of relief. Whew, she'd had a lucky escape there, she told herself. The last thing she wanted right now was a big fight. Or for her mum to go off on one of her guilt-fests and start blaming herself for failing her daughter by not being there enough. Jazmin hated it when that happened.

She could always handle her mum's anger – she could fight back, or walk away from it. What she couldn't deal with was the guilt thing. It never failed to upset her, that responsibility for someone else's pain.

Collecting her bag from the hallway, she toted it upstairs to her room. The least she could do in the circumstances was make a start on her homework, she decided. Or possibly make a start on making a start. She got out all her books and arranged them methodically in neat piles on her desk in an attempt to create the encouraging impression of a busy working environment.

Jazmin loved her room. It had taken some time and effort, but she'd finally got it just how she wanted it. The walls were painted deep, dark blue, a colour she had striven to get just right. It was the exact shade she associated with the depths of the ocean, a blue you could walk into and feel it moving gently all around you. There were big posters of black and white computer-generated fractals on two of the walls; she liked their patterned chaos, the beauty of their apparent randomness.

A small pine bookcase was crammed with crime fiction, while above her desk was her shelf of special things – a toy camel, a glass jar of coloured sand, her scented candle collection, some seashells picked up on a holiday beach, the china house from Prague and a picture of the father who had died of cancer while she was still a child. Jazmin lay down on her bed and folded her arms behind her head.

Ten minutes, she told herself, and then she'd *really* hit the books, promise.

She closed her eyes.

DOWNSTAIRS, ASSIA STIRRED CHEESE SAUCE AND SIGHED RESIGNEDLY. SHE GUESSED JAZMIN HAD SKIPPED SCHOOL. SHE ALSO KNEW THAT SHE WAS NOT GOING TO ADMIT IT. ASSIA considered her options: confrontation or complicity – and decided to cut herself some slack. She'd had a difficult and tiring day. She would accept Jazmin's very lame excuse and ignore what had happened. Right now, a big bust-up with her daughter was the last thing she needed, she told herself. What she needed was for their relationship to be good. For the lines of communication to remain open. Jazmin was an important link to Kirilovitch. It was essential for their relationship to continue.

Assia decanted the cooked cauliflower into a colander and rinsed it under the tap. She did not especially enjoy cooking, but recognized it as one of those daily things that patterned her life. Something she did without even thinking. She paused, holding the colander motionless over the sink, and stared into the middle distance as if suddenly transported to a place deep inside herself.

More and more, Assia was becoming convinced that there was some dark force that existed outside of and beyond human experience and that it had the power to wind itself, serpent-like, into the psyche of certain individuals. She felt that every assignment she undertook reinforced this. The knowledge preyed upon her mind. It preoccupied her, coming to her in her waking hours, when, like now, she was engaged upon some mindless task. It kept her awake at nights. And with it came the increasingly worrying feeling that she was powerless to protect those she loved and cared about.

"I THOUGHT WE'D INVITE OUR RUSSIAN VISITOR FOR DINNER TONIGHT," ASSIA REMARKED OVER BREAKFAST THE NEXT MORNING. HALF-AWAKE, AND ON AUTOMATIC PILOT, JAZMIN BLINKED at her. Then she shrugged. "Fine by me."

"I might even try to make some borsch for him. Help him to feel at home here."

"Some what?"

"It's soup, Russian-style. They make it out of beetroot."

"Eww! Gross!"

"I'm sure it will be delicious," her mum said firmly, although Jazmin did not think she sounded totally convinced.

Assia tidied the breakfast things and took them over to the dishwasher. She glanced down into the street. "Oh look, your homework friend is waiting for you," she said brightly.

Jazmin got up and peered over her shoulder. Zeb Stone

was once again leaning against the wall outside. She sighed, pulled a face, then caught the edge of her mum's expression. "What??" she demanded. "*What??*"

Assia shrugged her shoulders. "Nothing," she said innocently. "Nothing at all."

"Good," Jazmin growled, gulping down her juice, and cursing inwardly. Somehow – and she really wasn't sure how on earth it had happened – Zeb seemed to be under the completely mistaken impression that she was some sort of clever mathsy person, like he was.

She closed her eyes and groaned softly to herself. Once upon a time there was just Jaz Dawson, her glamorous crime-fighting alter-ego. Now, she was developing so many different personalities, she could start her own relay team.

She went upstairs to get ready for the day. Maybe if she stayed in the apartment long enough, Zeb would think she'd already left and go away. It was worth a try. She spent some time pottering around her room, rearranging bits and pieces. Then she went into the bathroom and stood in front of the mirror applying some more make-up. She stared at her reflection in the mirror, wondering for the gazillionth time why you couldn't put on mascara without having your mouth wide open.

Downstairs, Jazmin heard the familiar sound of her mum preparing to leave for work. She heard her call a cheerful goodbye up the stairs. Then the front door closed. A couple of seconds later, the sound of two people talking in the street drifted in through the open top window. Jazmin recognized her mum's voice. No prizes for guessing who the other person was then. So much for her cunning plan.

"Ah, *there* you are," Zeb greeted her happily when she finally and reluctantly emerged into the street. "Your mum said you'd be along in a minute."

"Yeah, she's kind of helpful like that," Jazmin observed caustically.

They set off together, Zeb loping down the road at super speed, Jazmin huffing along a couple of paces behind him, playing catch-up. "Hey, slow down a bit, will you!" she puffed as they came within sight of the learning centre gate. Obediently, Zeb slowed down and waited for her. Jazmin drew level, then stopped, pretending to check the books in her bag. In reality, she needed a couple of seconds to get her act together and tune her expression to something suitable before encountering the gate-girls.

"Hey, guess what? I've got double physics this morning," Zeb informed her happily while he waited for her to sort her stuff. Jazmin marvelled yet again at his weird ability to find rapture in learning. She'd rather eat worms. "Then I've got info tech and computing science," Zeb went on. "It's going to be a good day for me. How about you?"

Jazmin shrugged. Judging by the faces on the girls waiting outside the gate, she'd probably got a morning of whispered innuendo, bitchy remarks and spitefulness. It was not going to be a good day for her.

"Oh yeah – and before I forget, I have something for you," Zeb said. He swung his bag off his shoulder and took something out of one of the side pockets. "I picked it up in the library the other day. I thought you might like to come." He held out an A4 flyer. It was advertising a chess tournament. "It's going to be really amazing," Zeb continued enthusiastically. "Look – it says that anybody can enter. And do you see who's coming to judge it? Colle Kotronias! How about that?"

"Umm...yeah," Jazmin said, trying to assume an appropriately awed expression. "Looks good."

"I mean, how often do you get the chance to play in front of the under-twenty-one British champion?"

Given my level of ability, hopefully never, Jazmin thought to herself. "Thanks," she said, folding the flyer and stuffing it into her pocket, "I'll see what I'm doing and get back to you."

"I really hope you can come with me. I've followed all Colle's games," Zeb went on happily. "I was·actually at the London World Championship last year. I saw him play his final match. And do you know what he used?"

A chessboard? A chess set? His feet? Jazmin thought desperately. "Umm...no, I don't know," she admitted.

"He used the Sicilian Defence," Zeb announced triumphantly.

"Wow!"

"*But* he played the Sveshnikov Variation. How about that?"

"Yeah, I bet it kicked." Unh. So Zeb was also a chess freak. Why was she not surprised? It went so well with everything else about him.

Zeb gave her a nice smile and set off again towards the gate. Jazmin waited a couple of seconds. Then she took a deep breath, squared her shoulders, stuck her chin into the air and reminded herself that bad things only happen to bad people. Two seconds, she thought, and I can be the other side of this and safe inside the building.

As if it could ever be that easy.

"Hey, Jazmin, wait up!" Honi Delacy yelled out as she sailed by.

Jazmin stopped and waited. Because she chose to, she reminded herself. Meanwhile Honi shot a quick, significant look at her gang. Then she hurried over. Today, Jazmin noted, Honi was wearing another of her matchy pink outfits. She wore a lot of pink. Pink was Honi's *signature colour*. Jazmin smirked. Trying to get in touch with her inner moppet again, she thought sarkily. "Unh – what is it, Honi?" she asked, bestowing upon Honi a smile as warm as frostbite and bracing herself for the thuddage that was about to arrive.

Honi's eyes widened innocently. "There's no need to be so hostile, Jazmin," she said reproachfully, "I was only going to ask you to introduce me to Zeb."

"Oh...umm," Jazmin stuttered, taken aback. This was not what she'd been expecting. Feeling slightly awkward, she did the intro thing. Honi immediately flipped into her I'm-a-Total-Boy-Magnet persona. She tilted her head to one side, opened her eyes wide and began smiling up into Zeb's face. Zeb looked down at her, with a slightly bemused expression. Then he started talking to her politely.

Jazmin stood patiently by, waiting for Honi to get bored. But next thing, as if it had been prearranged, all Honi's friends suddenly came running across. They crowded round Honi and Zeb, creating a protective ring. Then they deliberately stood with their backs to Jazmin, freezing her out.

For a brief few seconds Jazmin stared at the row of unfriendly backs, taking in what had just happened. Then, clamping her lips together firmly, she turned and stalked up the steps into the learning centre. So that was what all that had been about. Well, mission accomplished. Honi Delacy had Got Her Man. As she always did. Even if she subsequently went through them like an arsonist through a hayfield.

Jazmin felt rage bubbling up hotly inside her. That girl was so good at pretending to be what she wasn't, she thought angrily. She was totally surfacy! All that cutesy gazing up and batting her eyelashes. It was like her body language was written in large print. But boys loved that sort of thing; they always got sucked in. And although Zeb was very clever, it was the wrong sort of cleverness: he was clever about stuff, not people. He would never see through Honi until it was too late.

Feeling extremely heart-of-darknessy, Jazmin slammed through the entrance door and rammed her card viciously into the registration slot. Sometime this morning, she was going to have to pull a Houdini and find an elsewhere to be, she thought. She really wasn't sure she could stand a whole day watching the unfolding of the Honi 'n' Zeb show.

LATER, IN ANOTHER PART OF THE CITY, THE RECEPTIONIST ON THE FRONT DESK OF THE MAYFAIR HOTEL, A DISCREET AND EXPENSIVE ESTABLISHMENT LOCATED IN A QUIET SIDE STREET JUST BEHIND Park Lane, handed the leather bound signing-in book to the latest guest.

"If you would just care to register, sir," she murmured.

The dark-haired and elegantly dressed man produced a solid silver Tiffany pen from his jacket pocket and began to fill in the page. The receptionist silently admired his handmade suit, silk shirt and tie, the Rolex watch on his left wrist, and the matching Louis Vuitton luggage just brought in from the taxi by the doorman, and now waiting to be taken up to the suite of rooms on the fourth floor. Everything about this guest spoke of affluence and good taste. Exactly the kind of client that the hotel catered for.

"And are you visiting London for business, or for pleasure, sir?" she asked politely.

The man signed his name with an extravagant flourish, giving her a dazzling white-toothed smile. "Are they not the same thing?" he said. His voice betrayed the faint trace of a foreign accent.

The receptionist blushed and handed the key to the room to the bellboy. The man pocketed his pen and walked swiftly across the lush crimson-carpeted lobby to the lift. The receptionist glanced down at the completed page: *Ivan Petrov*, she read, followed by a Moscow address. A rich Russian. Well. They did not get many of those staying at this hotel. Usually the Russians preferred to stay at the Dorchester or the Ritz. Somewhere larger, more public and showy.

She glanced up, just in time to see the lift doors closing. The receptionist closed the book and replaced it in its pigeonhole behind her desk. Then she went to make herself a cup of coffee. Whatever the reason for Mr. Petrov's visit, or his slightly unusual choice of hotel, she reminded herself, it really was none of her business, was it?

MEANWHILE ASSIA HAD TAKEN A LONG LUNCH BREAK AND GONE SHOPPING FOR HER DINNER PARTY. AFTER CONSULTING A COUPLE OF RECIPE SITES ON THE INTERNET, SHE HAD FINALLY DECIDED TO DO a roast with fresh vegetables, roast potatoes and gravy.

And to follow, apple crumble and custard. A traditional English meal. There seemed little point in trying to imitate the cuisine the Russian had grown up with. Her attempts would never come up to scratch. And the chances of Jazmin eating it were remote in the extreme. Assia wanted the evening to go well, and the thought of her daughter poking her food around with a fork and pulling disgusted faces was not part of the plan. Plain English food was best and safest in the long run, she thought to herself, as she loaded up her cart.

ONCE AGAIN JAZMIN HAD SPENT ANOTHER DAY ON HER OWN HANGING OUT IN THE LIBRARY. IT WAS BECOMING A BIT OF A HABIT. AS SOON AS SHE GOT BACK HOME LATER THAT AFTERNOON, SHE went straight upstairs to her room and hunted around in the back of her closet. Jazmin had recently inherited a bag of her rich cousin Clea's cast-off clothes.

Most of them were black.

Jazmin didn't wear a lot of black, which was why the clothes had been left in a bag at the back of her wardrobe, but now seemed like a good moment to bring them out. After her brush with Destructo Girl, black fitted perfectly with the way she was feeling. She could be blue in black.

"You look very...different," Assia said a short while later as Jazmin entered the kitchen. "I don't think I've ever seen you wear black before." She cut her daughter a curious look. "Any reason for the change?"

For a fleeting moment, Jazmin contemplated sharing with her mum that her life had suddenly gone pear-shaped, but she reminded herself sternly that however appealing it might seem, it was never a good idea to confide in a parent: it would always come back to you. To deflect attention from herself, she sniffed the cooking smells emanating from the oven and asked: "Smells nice. What's for dinner? You haven't done that beetroot thing, have you?"

"It's a plain roast," Assia told her. "I thought I'd keep it nice and simple." She checked the time. "I have to go and collect Mr. Smith now," she said, picking up her car keys from the table. "Can you keep an eye on the meal for me? Just check in the oven every now and then and make sure the beef's not burning."

"Will do. Hey, hope he's not a vegetarian, eh?" Jazmin joked.

Her mum turned round to face her, an expression of dismay on her face. "Oh no – you know, I never even asked him!"

"Hey, relax, Mum, don't stress, it'll be fine," Jazmin reassured her. "He'll love it."

"I hope so. Well, I'll see you shortly." Assia walked towards the kitchen door, paused in the doorway, turned, gave her daughter another searching top-to-toe look and left.

Jazmin leaned against the kitchen counter and stared

mournfully out of the window, deciding that the dark sky chimed in perfectly with her dark mood. She was beginning to regret that when she'd first met Zeb Stone, she'd been so quick to decide he was a boring geeky nerd and that they had absolutely nothing in common. Because now, the more she thought about Zeb, the more she began to realize that actually he possessed plenty of good points. He was interested in her, he seemed to enjoy her company, and best of all, he actually thought she was as clever as he was.

Nobody had ever thought Jazmin was super-intelligent before. It was very flattering. Zeb had potential. How come she hadn't seen all this? she wondered, as she continued staring at the gloomy sky. And how come she was only seeing it now, when she'd lost him to Honi Delacy, a girl who thought rearranging her nail polish collection was an intellectual activity?

Jazmin sighed. Then she wrinkled her nose. What was that horrible smell? She glanced down. Smoke was coming from the oven. Uh-oh. She whipped the door open and surveyed the burned joint of beef. Darn. She'd been so busy thinking about her life that she'd neglected her culinary duties. Now she had a major catering crisis on her hands. She reached for the oven gloves and lifted the roasting tray onto the counter. She needed to saw off the black bits before her mum got back and discovered what she'd done.

"ANOTHER SLICE OF BEEF?" ASSIA ASKED KIRILOVITCH. "JAZMIN – HAVE SOME MORE ROAST POTATOES, I CAN'T BELIEVE YOU'VE ONLY EATEN ONE."

Jazmin poked her food around with her fork and shook her head.

Assia raised her eyebrows questioningly. "It's unlike you to turn down roast potatoes. Are you feeling all right, hon?"

Jazmin felt her cheeks going red with embarrassment. "I'm fine, Mum. Don't fuss," she muttered.

"Well, I should like some more, Assia," Kirilovitch cut in, holding out his plate. "It's delicious. I can't remember when I last enjoyed a home-cooked meal like this!"

He looked across the table at Jazmin and winked. Despite herself, Jazmin found she was grinning back. She was starting to like the old man, she thought. And he'd certainly gone to some trouble to smarten himself up for his evening out. Navy suit, crisp white shirt and a red and yellow striped tie. Since she'd last seen him, he'd had a haircut, and his iron-grey hair was now neatly combed back from his forehead. It made him look completely different – kind of elderly professor rather than scruffy old senior, she thought.

Also he'd trimmed back his moustache, which gave his face a less fierce, hawkish expression. And he'd brought flowers: a big bunch for her mum and, unbelievably, a small bunch of freesias for her. "For my two gracious hostesses," he'd said, making a bow as he handed them over on the doorstep. Jazmin had been so surprised, she'd nearly dropped hers on the carpet. Nobody had ever given her a bunch of flowers before.

Assia refilled Kirilovitch's plate. He ate hungrily.

"So," Assia asked, refocusing her attention upon her daughter so that the old man could finish his food in peace, "how was the learning centre today?"

Jazmin cut her meat into tiny segments and arranged them into a pattern. "Yeah, well, you know," she shrugged nonchalantly. Once again she caught the old man's eyes; another look of complicity passed between them.

"Did you get all your homework finished?" Assia pursued.

"Err, sort of."

"Define 'sort of'."

Jazmin pulled a face. Honestly! What was with all the questioning? If they ever made interrogation an Olympic sport, her mum could represent England, she thought disgustedly. She sighed exaggeratedly. "It's ongoing, all right?"

As soon as the meal was over, Assia steered their guest to a comfortable chair in the living room. "Shall we have some music with our coffee?" she asked him.

The old man nodded. "That would be nice."

Assia went over to the music centre and stood thinking. "Let me see, what would be good? Yes, I think this is the right piece," she said, pressing a button. She returned to her chair. There was a pause, then the room was filled with the swirling sound of violins.

"Ah. Tchaikovsky," Kirilovitch murmured. He settled back into his chair with a deep and contented sigh and closed his eyes. Assia folded her arms in her lap and leaned back, her eyes closing too. Jazmin slid into a chair and got ready for the interesting revelations to start. She knew from the books she'd read and the movies she'd seen that the best conversations always happened after dinner. Food and wine loosened people's tongues so that they felt relaxed. Then they talked. Often indiscreetly. Things were admitted that should not have been. After-dinner conversations were a source of rich pickings for the judicial listener.

Jazmin waited for a while, but to her disappointment, the adults just went on sitting in their chairs with their eyes shut. This was no good, she thought. They ought to be talking animatedly, her mum probing gently, asking searching questions, until the old man finally told her the whole story of the clinic and what he knew about it. She waited a couple more minutes, then pointedly cleared her throat. "So," she said conversationally, "what shall we talk about?"

Assia opened one eye and put a finger to her lips.

Jazmin glared at her, but Assia had already closed her eyes again. She waited a bit longer to see if the probing questions were about to start, then gave in. This was boring. Nothing was happening. "Right, I'm going up to my room," she announced. There was no response. Her mum's eyes remained tightly shut. The old man's mouth had fallen slightly open. He was breathing loudly and seemed to have fallen asleep. Jazmin rolled her eyes and sighed. Sheesh! Even homework was more exciting than this. She got up and tiptoed quietly out of the lounge.

BACK IN HER ROOM ONCE MORE, JAZMIN SAT DOWN AT HER DESK AND CHECKED HER HOMEWORK DIARY. THEN SHE OPENED UP HER BOOKS AND STARTED STUDYING. SHE WAS GOING TO HAVE TO WATCH out, she thought to herself, as she started to fill in a chart on French irregular verbs. It looked like her mum was about to embark on one of her periodic "showing an interest" phases.

There was also another good reason to hit the books. Several of her facilitators had threatened to contact her parent about the amount of work she wasn't doing. Her science facilitator had already taken it to the next level – Jazmin'd recently intercepted a letter from him complaining about the absence of homework. Naturally, she'd torn up the letter and binned it before her mum could see it, but she had a nasty feeling that it wouldn't be the last one.

Three-quarters of an hour passed. Jazmin completed the French chart, then wrote a couple of paragraphs assessing

Macbeth's potential as a tragic hero. Twice, she crept out onto the landing and listened. No snatches of conversation were drifting up from the living room. What were they doing down there – hibernating? Finally, when she could study no longer, she closed her books and sat staring out of her window for a bit to rest her brain.

Thinking back on her nasty day, Jazmin was forced to admit that she was still upset about what had happened. She was still furious at how easily Honi had taken Zeb away from her. And how casually he had just transferred his friendship from her to Honi. Well, he needn't think he could come running back, she thought indignantly. If he preferred to hang out with Ms. Retail Therapy Queen, that was fine. He'd had his chance to be her friend, and he'd blown it.

Suddenly snatching up the leaflet Zeb had given her earlier, Jazmin scrumpled it into a ball and threw it across the room. So much for Zeb and his stupid chess competition! Then she paused. The chess competition had struck a sudden chord. Okay, so maybe she personally wouldn't be seen dead at it, but she knew somebody who'd probably like to go. She picked up the leaflet, smoothed it out again and went downstairs.

The old man read slowly through the flyer. His eyes brightened. "This looks interesting," he said. "I haven't had a good game of chess for a while." He checked the date of the event, then handed the flyer to Assia to look at.

"And funnily enough, I don't think I have anything planned for this Saturday," he said, giving her a dry smile. "Thank you, I'd love to go."

Assia scanned the leaflet, then gave her daughter an approving glance. "This is really thoughtful of you, hon," she smiled.

Jazmin shrugged modestly. She felt validated. She'd done a good deed in a nasty world. The old man was going to have a nice time playing chess, her mum was pleased with her, and with a bit of luck, she'd scored a Saturday morning lazing in bed.

"So what time should she call for you?" Assia asked.

What? Jazmin's smug smile wiped itself off her face.

"Maybe nine o'clock? What do you think?"

"Umm...hang on. I wasn't...I mean..." Jazmin tried to interrupt, but neither of them was paying her any attention.

"Right you are then," Assia agreed. "She'll be with you at nine."

"I'll look forward to it."

Jazmin stared at them both in dismay.

"Ready to go?" Assia asked the old man.

"Yes, I'm ready."

Assia took him by the arm. "See you later," she called over her shoulder as the two of them headed out into the hallway. At the front door, Kirilovitch turned and gave Jazmin a big melty smile. "Thank you for your company tonight, Jazmin," he said. "And I'm really looking forward to our trip together."

"Oh, err...hey, that's fine," Jazmin stammered, going bright red. *Just fine,* she thought grimly to herself, as the front door closed on them. Unh. How had this come about? Turning up at the chess competition would send out totally the wrong message to Zeb. It'd say she was still a friend. It was so not what she wanted to happen.

THE OLD MAN UNLOCKED HIS FRONT DOOR AND LET HIMSELF INTO THE SMALL HOUSE. HE HAD ENJOYED VISITING ASSIA DAWSON AND HER DAUGHTER, ENJOYED IT VERY MUCH. THEY HAD *DUSHA,* SOUL, HE thought. And it was certainly kind of Jazmin to take him out on Saturday. Nevertheless it was good to be able to close his own door, to be alone again, to think about the past.

He sat down in the comfortable chair. A miew from the bedroom heralded the arrival of the cat. It paused for a second, staring meditatively up at him with its clear amber eyes, before launching itself onto his lap, where it circled a couple of times, then settled down, purring gently.

Extending a hand, he stroked the soft black fur. Then he closed his eyes. First came images of the day. He let them pass. Next, etched into the retinal grain behind his eyelids, he saw two figures. A woman and a small child. They were wearing long woollen coats, warm knitted hats. They walked towards him through the snow, their eyes bright and alive, cheeks red with the cold. The little one clung tightly to the woman's hand.

The old man held his grief at bay, refusing to give in to sorrow. It was not yet time. Grief was a gift, he reminded himself, something you had to earn, and there were still unfinished things he had to do. Then and only then, could he finally make peace with the past.

SATURDAY MORNING DAWNED FINE AND DRY. ASSIA KNOCKED GENTLY ON JAZMIN'S BEDROOM DOOR. WHEN THERE WAS NO REPLY, SHE OPENED IT AND, CARRYING THE TRAY, ADVANCED TOWARDS THE bed where a silent, motionless shape under the duvet was the scant evidence of human life.

"Morning, hon. Time to wake up," she said to the shape, which muttered incoherently to itself for a bit while it made the short journey into consciousness. Then Jazmin's head emerged, tousled and bleary-eyed. "Wha...?" she blurred sleepily.

"It's eight o'clock. I brought you breakfast in bed."

Jazmin levered herself upright at once. Breakfast in bed? Unheard of! She made a space for the tray and surveyed the contents. Fresh orange juice in her special blue and white mug, white toast, butter and her favourite ginger marmalade.

"This looks very nice," she said. She shot her mum a suspicious look. "Am I ill or something?"

Her mum laughed. "I thought you deserved it. Giving up your Saturday to take our Russian friend to the chess tournament."

"Oh. That." Jazmin's face fell. She sagged against her pillow. She had forgotten all about the chess tournament. For a fleeting moment, she had thought that the breakfast was a treat, the prelude to a lazy day.

Her mum smiled down at her. "You enjoy your breakfast, and when you're ready, I'll give you both a lift," she said.

Jazmin sat bolt upright once more. "*What?* Hello – I can walk. I'm not seven years old!" she protested indignantly.

"I do know that. Nevertheless, I'm still driving you both there. And I'll pick you up later."

A sudden awful vision floated before Jazmin's eyes: she saw Honi Delacy and Zeb Stone standing outside the library, hand in hand, watching her getting out of her mother's car. They were laughing at her.

"Sorry, I am so not going anywhere in your car," she stated firmly. "Do you know what people will think?"

Her mum turned in the doorway. "I haven't a clue what people will think, but I'm sure you can rise above it," she said drily. "So finish your breakfast, get dressed and I'll wait for you downstairs."

JAZMIN AND THE OLD MAN STOOD IN THE QUEUE WAITING TO REGISTER FOR THE TOURNAMENT. THE RUSSIAN WAS CARRYING A BOX OF CHESS PIECES UNDER ONE ARM, AND HIS FACE WORE AN expression of eager expectation. He was clearly looking forward to the event. Jazmin, in contrast, was trying to recce the room while keeping her head down. She was checking to see if Zeb had arrived. And if Honi was with him. Although she speculated that if Honi was going to turn up, it wouldn't be until later. Much later. Nine fifteen on a Saturday morning was far too early for a shoppy girl like Honi Delacy. After all, the mall didn't open until ten. Jazmin reckoned she'd want to put in a couple of hours of retail therapy exercising her paycard before she did anything else.

Kirilovitch registered himself, remembering to use his new English name, and they walked into the library hall, where tables and time clocks had been set up ready for the contestants. "We may as well sit down," the old man said. "They won't make the draw for a while."

"Let's go sit at the back," Jazmin said firmly. She led the way to the rear of the hall, instantly regretting her decision as she saw who was sitting on the end of the back row, a chess box on his lap.

"Hey, Jazmin! Great, you made it," Zeb said, his face breaking into a smile of recognition and welcome. He got to his feet to allow her to squeeze through.

Jazmin glared at him. She stalked past, managing to

kick him hard in the ankle as she did so. "My word, clumsy old me," she said innocently.

Wincing, Zeb sat down again. "It's going to be a good competition," he said, seeming oblivious to the large iceberg towering over him. "Have you registered yet? Hey, maybe we'll get to play each other – that'd be fun, wouldn't it? And this must be your granddad?"

Jazmin dried. Suddenly she couldn't think of a single way to introduce the Russian that didn't involve getting herself into complicated explanations. Fortunately, the old man came to her rescue.

"Nearly right. I'm her Great-Uncle Charles," he said smoothly, sitting down next to Zeb and holding out his hand. "I'm here for a short visit."

"Yeah – from abroad," Jazmin put in quickly.

Zeb shook Kirilovitch's hand. "Good to meet you," he said, glancing from the old man's face to Jazmin's. He nodded thoughtfully. "Yup, I can definitely see the family resemblance."

Jazmin gaped at him in astonishment. "You can?"

"It's your foreheads," Zeb went on, nodding happily. "Same shape."

"They are?"

"And your eyes too."

"Oh really?"

"I'm quite observant," Zeb continued, totally oblivious to the amused glances being exchanged behind his back.

"I notice things about people."

"You do?" Jazmin cut her eyes at the old man, who gave her a secret wink.

Zeb settled back in his chair with a satisfied air. "Well, I've just been speaking to Colle Kotronias," he told them both. "In a minute, he's going to talk us all through one of his championship games while they make the draw for the first round."

Sure enough, a tall, dark-haired, serious young man wearing black-rimmed glasses was moving to stand in front of a big electronic screen. People began hurrying to find seats. Colle Kotronias introduced himself and started talking animatedly.

"Ah, this looks like the Paris Open last July," Kirilovitch remarked happily, settling back comfortably in his seat as the screen lit up to display the opening moves of the game.

Zeb turned to him. "You recognize it?"

"Yes, I was in the audience."

Zeb's expression was seraphic. "Amazing," he breathed. "Jazmin never mentioned she had a great-uncle who was as interested in chess as she is."

The old man assumed a nonchalant expression. "I guess she had better things to talk about," he said innocently. Jazmin cut him a sharp look; he turned his head slightly, and their eyes met. "Thanks," she mouthed. He shrugged. Jazmin glanced past him at Zeb to see whether he had noticed, but his attention was now totally focused on the screen. "You're good at pretending to be someone else, aren't you?" she muttered under her breath. The old man gave her a wry smile, "I should be: I've had quite a lot of practice over the years," he said quietly.

As soon as the under-twenty-one champion had finished speaking, one of the competition organizers stepped up to the microphone and, after explaining the rules, began to announce the draws for the first round. Zeb's name was called early on. Jazmin was relieved. She didn't want him to realize she was not actually taking part in the competition. (Although Mr. Observant didn't seem to have spotted her lack of a chess set, she noted.) Now with a bit of luck, she could pretend she was knocked out in the first round, but was trying to be brave about it.

"Will you stay and watch?" Kirilovitch asked her.

"Sure. I promised Mum I'd take you to the competition," Jazmin replied dutifully.

The old man gave her a mischievous smile. "I don't remember you promising to stay, though," he said. "And there are some very nice shops out there in the mall, aren't there? I bet you'd rather go and look round for a while?"

Jazmin hesitated. "I don't know. I think I'm supposed to be keeping an eye on you."

"Nothing's going to happen to me here," the old man said drily. He held out his left wrist. "And of course I have my wonderful watch to protect me if it does." He smiled at her. "You go and enjoy yourself. Maybe we could meet up for lunch. Unless, of course..." And he nodded to where Zeb and another competitor were setting up their board ready for the first game.

Jazmin eye-rolled. "Oh, *puh-leease*! Not you too."

"Lunch it is then," he said, getting to his feet to let her pass. "Have a nice morning," he added.

Jazmin nodded. "Okay, if you're sure, I'll see you back here at one," she said gratefully. She headed quickly for the main exit.

OUT IN THE MAIN MALL, ALL OF THE SHOPS WERE IN FULL-ON CHRISTMAS MODE. THERE WERE BOXES OF TINSEL AND SHINY BAUBLES STACKED BY COUNTERS. RACKS OF CHRISTMAS CARDS were everywhere, accompanied by rolls of gold and silver wrapping. A large indoor ice-rink had been built on the ground floor, and giant ropes of red and green and silver fairy lights had been strung across the wide atrium ceilings. Jazmin couldn't resist a tiny buzz of excitement: she always liked Christmas and all its many rituals.

Every year she and her granddad would choose a tree for the apartment and then decorate it together. Last year, she had also helped him do a tree for his new home in the retirement community. This year however, it would all be different, she thought with a slight pang of regret: her granddad had gone to spend the holiday with her cousin

Clea and her family, which meant she'd have to choose just one tree and decorate it all on her own.

Jazmin strolled around window-shopping for a while, then decided to try out one of the many snack bars. She picked up a tray and selected an apple and cinnamon scone and some juice. She paid for her food and carried it over to a single table. She was a serial snacker, she thought to herself proudly as she sat down. It was an accomplishment; not everybody could do it.

When Jazmin eventually returned to the competition, she found Kirilovitch sitting on a chair, patiently waiting for her to arrive. Zeb was still playing. A different opponent this time.

"I enjoyed that," the old man said happily. He eased himself stiffly out of his seat.

"Did you win?"

"One win, one draw, and I have one more match this afternoon. Your friend is a very good chess player, isn't he? I've been watching him for the last fifteen minutes."

"Yeah?" Jazmin said. "There's a good sandwich place on the top floor of the library," she went on. "We can eat there."

Jazmin led the way out of the hall. She was already mind-stacking all the questions she wanted to ask him over lunch. She pushed open the glass doors and entered the main library building itself. The old man followed her obediently, but stopped once he'd stepped inside. "Ah, a library," he breathed, looking all around him. "Books." The expression on his face reminded Jazmin irresistibly of a dog that had just spotted a rabbit. He started to drift towards the shelves. "There's something about being surrounded by books," he continued dreamily. "It makes you feel...safe. When I lived in Paris, I spent quite a lot of time in libraries."

"Actually, I spend quite a lot of time in this one," Jazmin told him wryly. "Do you want to look round? You can check out a book."

The old man turned to face her. "Really?" he asked eagerly. "Are you sure?"

Jazmin nodded. She fumbled in her bag and held out her card. "Here, borrow my card. I'll just be over there," she said, indicating the carousel of crime fiction. "You take as long as you like. Then we'll have some lunch."

JAZMIN AND KIRILOVITCH CARRIED THEIR TRAYS TO A QUIET CORNER TABLE AND SAT DOWN. THEY ATE IN SILENCE FOR A WHILE. THEN JAZMIN LEANED FORWARD IN HER SEAT. "SO," SHE SAID. "THERE was a man in a Mercedes who recognized you. Nikolai Arkady – isn't that his name? You were in Paris, weren't you? What's the deal with him?"

The old man eyed her. "You ask a lot of questions, don't you?" he grumbled good-naturedly.

"Yes, I do," Jazmin agreed.

"Should I be talking to you about this?"

"Why not?"

"I'm not sure your mother would approve."

Jazmin waved her hand airily. "Hey, I help out all the time. Last summer, I was working with her in Prague. I'm not on the payroll *officially*, but I'm an essential part of the team." She cut him a wide, innocent smile, while silently reassuring herself that not telling the truth was not the same as lying.

Kirilovitch sighed.

"I already know why the ISA want to get hold of him – they think he might try to intimidate witnesses," Jazmin said, precising a bit more of the conversation she'd overheard her mum having. (She learned a lot from sitting on the top stair late at night with the landing light off.) "They're still trying to track him down, aren't they?"

Kirilovitch smiled thinly. "Best of luck to them," he said. "If Nikolai doesn't want to be found, he won't be. He's cunning, like a fox. I used to play chess with him when I lived in Russia. He won every game. One time, I remember getting angry and accusing him of cheating; he told me he would always win because he could always think further ahead than I could."

"So where do you think he is now?"

Kirilovitch shrugged. "He's probably gone to ground somewhere. Rome, Berlin, Hong Kong, he has business contacts all over the world. He'll stay hidden until the heat's off. They'll never catch him." He glanced at his watch. "Ah – I think we'd better be getting back," he said. "I don't want to keep my opponent waiting."

Disappointed she hadn't learned more about his past, Jazmin led the old man back to the hall, where a small serious kid with wire-rimmed glasses was already sitting at the table waiting impatiently for their game to begin. She slid into a seat and watched them go through their opening moves. It was very quiet in the hall, warm too. Audience and players were all focused on the various chessboards. A press reporter was talking to Kotronias and the organizer. Jazmin tried to focus, but after a while, her eyelids began to get heavy and she started yawning. Watching chess was about as exciting as snail racing, she thought, as her eyes slowly closed, and her head nodded gently forwards.

She was woken up by somebody shaking her vigorously by the shoulder. Jazmin opened her eyes. Her mum was bending over her, her face alive with amusement. "Sleeping on the job!" she scolded. "Oh dear, oh dear – whatever are you like?"

Jazmin rubbed her eyes and stared around the hall. Some of the contestants had gone. The audience were still watching while the last few pairs finished their games. Kirilovitch was sitting a few seats away, waiting patiently for her to wake up.

"Unh – I am so sorry," Jazmin apologized, going bright scarlet with embarrassment.

"No problem," said the old man mildly. "You didn't miss much – I've just been beaten by a ten-year-old. Very humiliating!"

Assia straightened up. "Ready to go, everybody?"

The old man picked up his box of chess pieces. "*Atleechna*," he sighed. "That was excellent."

Jazmin stretched her arms above her head, rubbed her eyes and gave the room a quick scope. As if reading her thoughts, he said: "I'm afraid you missed your friends, but they all said to say hello."

"My friends?"

"Zeb and the two girls."

Jazmin's heart lurched uncomfortably. "What two girls?"

The old man frowned. "I didn't catch their names. They arrived while you were sleeping. One of them had fair hair. The other one—"

"Had long plaits with beads," Jazmin finished.

"That's right. They all left together about ten minutes ago."

Jazmin stared blankly at him while the full implications of what he had just said hit her like a sockful of wet cement. Argh! No-no-no! She had been caught fast asleep in public by Terminator Barbie and her Evil Sidekick! She tried and failed to fight her rising horror. What if her mouth was wide open? she thought frantically. What if she had been drooling?

Jazmin followed her mum and Kirilovitch out of the hall. She knew she was never going to live this down! She had handed her enemies a loaded gun, and they were going to use it on her. Hello and Goodbye, Life, she thought gloomily as she trailed out to the car park. She was so going to suffer for this on Monday morning.

JAZMiN SLEPT iN ON SUNDAY. BY THE TiME SHE FiNALLY SURFACED, THE APARTMENT WAS EMPTY. HER MUM HAD GONE OUT, LEAViNG HER A NOTE ON THE KiTCHEN TABLE: *AM TAKING OUR friend for tour of London and chat. Back later. Mum X.*

Double darn, Jazmin thought as she prepared herself a late breakfast. She'd've really liked to have gone with them. There hadn't been much time yesterday to Sherlock. But she also knew that for her mum, the clock was ticking. Her department had several cases on the go right now, and she wanted to put this one to bed as soon as possible.

Jazmin took her breakfast back upstairs to her room to eat. She noticed that her micro was flashing on her desk. Someone must've sent her a message while she was downstairs. She flipped the lid open, then sat and watched with a sinking heart as the screen filled up with ZZZZZs.

Hell Week had begun early.

ASSIA HAD PARKED THE CAR FACING THE THAMES BARRIER. IT WAS A FINE, SUNNY MORNING WITH A BRIGHT SKY. GULLS LAZED AND QUARRELLED ON UPDRAUGHTS, AND THE RIVER WAS A GENTLY rippling carpet. Assia and Kirilovitch sat next to each other for a while, watching the sun painting silver streaks onto the surface of the water. Cars were like confessionals, she thought. Partly it was the sense of closeness without facing each other. Partly it was the sense of being in transit; nothing counted.

She switched on her digital recorder.

"So tell me about your work at the Arkadia Clinic," she said.

The old man sighed deeply. He stared out over the river wall, pushing back the hair which had fallen, like shiny strands of metal, onto his forehead. After a few seconds of silence, Assia turned off the recorder. "You said you would talk to us if we relocated you, Ivan Kirilovitch," she said evenly. "We have kept our side of the agreement. Now it's time for you to keep yours."

The old man stared out of the windscreen, his face a blank. "You think it's that easy, do you?" he murmured. "You think going back to the past is like walking in the park?"

There was another silence. They watched the birds swooping low over the grey-green water.

"Talk to me," Assia said.

"What shall I talk about?"

Assia leaned across and momentarily covered his hand with hers. "Why don't we start with Boris Arkady?" she said, switching on the recorder once more. "You've told me very little about him. Tell me some more. What was he really like underneath?"

There was another long pause. Then the old man began speaking. "You never believe that people can be entirely cold," he said slowly. "In the hardest of hearts, there has to be some warmth somewhere. After all, even hatred has warmth, if you think about it. But with Boris Arkady, the normal rules didn't apply. Under the charm and the smiles, he was cold in a way I've never experienced before. Wherever he was, he filled the space around him with an overwhelming current of cold energy. Many times I tried to picture him as a child, tried to find something human and understandable about him, something I could relate to. But I never could. All I knew was that I began by admiring him, and then I feared him. And that fear got greater as the years passed."

He stared down at the rope-like veins on the back of his hands, then turned to face Assia. "And in answer to the question you've been dying to ask – yes, I knew about the organ trafficking. It was impossible to fulfil the clinic's website boast that it could obtain 'the healthiest young organs from hard-working people, many of them vegetarians and all in the best of health' solely from donations. I suspected most of the organs we used had to come from the black market."

Assia nodded. At last. Finally, they were getting to the reason why the old man was here. "You knew, and it didn't worry you?"

Kirilovitch gave a harsh laugh. "Only when I thought about it. And over the eighteen years that I worked with Arkady, I tried not to think about it too often, because I was earning a lot of money, living a very good life, you see. And I was married to a wonderful woman. Who just happened to be my boss's daughter. Compared to my time in Moscow, working at the Arkadia Clinic was like being in Paradise.

"And Arkady – he could twist things so persuasively. He used to describe himself as a 'benevolent entrepreneur'. He offered people a second chance at life. Maybe the second chance had a huge price tag attached to it, but that was no problem for the rich international clientele the clinic catered for. And maybe it involved the suffering or death of some poor person thousands of miles away, but..." he shrugged, "that was none of our business. Oh yes, Boris Arkady could be very convincing, if you wanted to be convinced." The old man shrugged deprecatingly. "And I'm afraid that in those days I did," he confessed with a sigh.

There was another silence. Then, just as Assia was about to switch off the digital recorder, Kirilovitch cleared his throat. "So, how did you find out what was going on?" he asked.

"By accident," Assia said. "Ironic really. A young

German girl was in a road accident – she was taken to a Berlin hospital, but died of her injuries two days later. When the hospital authorities finally released her to her parents for burial, the mother noticed some unusual marks on her daughter's body. She arranged for an autopsy to be done privately, but when the doctor opened the body, to his shock and surprise, he found nothing there – all the major organs had been taken. The poor dead girl was nothing but an empty shell. The German media picked up the story immediately – there was a huge public outcry. The surgeon at the original hospital was investigated. And one thing led to another."

The old man sat motionless, listening intently.

"Of course, it was not the first time that such things had happened," Assia went on. "There had been other cases of transplant tourism, as it's called. But nothing on the scale of this. Europe, India, the Far East, even Mexico. Everywhere, the authorities started hearing gruesome tales of organ trafficking. Healthy poor people being forced to sell their organs. The newly dead stripped of their body parts. A huge international black market. And that was where we came in. Something that efficient and well-organized had to have a person behind it. A Mr. Big. The ISA was tasked with finding him."

"And you found him."

"We did. Although it has taken us a long time. People kept 'disappearing' just as we were about to question them. Nobody from the clinic would talk to us. They still won't. But now, with what our teams have already uncovered and with your statement as back-up, we should be able to stop Boris Arkady once and for all."

Kirilovitch's lips moved silently. Then he shook his head firmly. "No, you won't," he said firmly. "He will slip out of your grasp. Whatever evidence you present, you will never entrap him. He is like a wise old wolf – he has lived in the forest far too long, and he is much too clever to be caught by the huntsman's tricks."

Assia clicked her teeth. "If you believe that, why on earth did you agree to help us in the first place?" she remarked irritably.

There was a silence.

The old man went on staring out of the front windscreen.

Then, "I agreed for one reason only," he said. "I want to see my wife and daughter again. I want my life back. I have spent ten years waiting for this moment. Ten years of living in the shadows, always looking over my shoulder, never having the chance to get justice for myself and what happened to me. But now suddenly, the opportunity has arrived."

Kirilovitch turned to face Assia. "So, this is the deal," he said crisply. "First, you will find my family, wherever they are. And in return," he continued, "I will give you my copy of Boris Arkady's secret computer file – which you all clearly know nothing about – because, believe me, that is the only thing that will guarantee he never walks this earth as a free man again."

Assia sucked in her breath. Kirilovitch sat composedly, his hands in his lap. His face was expressionless as he stared at her, waiting calmly for her response. In the silence that followed, the only sound was a click as Assia leaned forward and switched off the digital recorder.

ASSIA DROPPED THE OLD MAN BACK AT THE RETIREMENT COMMUNITY. THEN SHE DROVE HER CAR TO PARLIAMENT HILL FIELDS AND PARKED IN A SIDE ROAD. SHE NEEDED A CHANGE OF scene and a chance to stretch her legs. She also needed to find a quiet place to sit and gather her thoughts before going home. She set off up the hill at a brisk walking pace. Reaching the summit, she sat down on one of the benches and gazed at the city skyline, trying to get her head around what she had just learned.

Assia admitted to herself that Kirilovitch's revelation about the computer file had shocked her deeply. What had also come as a shock was the discovery that she and her organization were pawns in somebody else's game. That there were two agendas here: the ISA's and Kirilovitch's. Now, the Russian had suddenly shifted the goalposts. He had initiated a new game, and she was going to have to play by his rules.

Assia thought about the conversation that had just taken place. What Kirilovitch had revealed to her had tapped into that feeling she so often felt, of the dark shadows that crept up the underside of the world. She wondered whether one could ever truly know another person. She had thought she was beginning to get close to the Russian. Now she admitted to herself that she had been wrong. She had only got to know the part of him on the surface, the bit he'd carefully chosen for her to see. Underneath there was a whole vast area of his life that he had kept hidden.

All around Assia, people swirled past, enjoying their Sunday, getting on with the business of their lives. Parents pushed children in strollers, their small bodies muffled up against the biting cold. Rich local residents walked their pampered pooches. Young couples strolled past, hand in hand. The ubiquitous lone jogger panted by. Assia found herself staring fixedly at each of their faces. Asking herself questions about them. About what she saw, and what she could not see. The surfaces and the shadows, and the secrets that lay hidden deep inside.

As soon as Assia's car had driven off, Kirilovitch had gone into the kitchen to make himself a snack. The cat, an ever-empty stomach on paws, presented itself hopefully at its bowl. He bent down and stroked the furry top of its head. Then he filled the cat's bowl with food. Maybe he should have waited a bit longer, he debated with himself. And yet, what choice did he have? Dealing with these people, however pleasant they seemed, was always like a game of chess. One in which you can anticipate nothing other than the fact that your opponent is probably two moves ahead of you. And at his back, there was that other opponent, who had always been several moves ahead.

The old man opened the scrapbook inside his head. He saw a cold Siberian night in the depths of winter; his car speeding along the highway. Was it his imagination, or did he catch the glimpse of headlights in his driving mirror just before his brakes failed and his car shot off the road? He flashed back to the frozen forest, the crackle of flames. And as he dragged himself out of the burning car, had he seen in his peripheral vision the hooded figure of a man running quickly from the scene?

Maybe. Whatever the truth was, he had done the right thing, he told himself, switching on the kettle and placing a spoonful of jam in the cup. Another game of chess, one that had been being played for a very long time, was now entering its endgame. Now he remembered the computer screen flickering gently in the darkened room. The soft voice of menace at his shoulder. The glint of the shiny steel paper knife on the desk. *I should have finished him off while I had the chance*, he thought fiercely. There was nobody in the building. No witnesses.

Regret. The eighth deadly sin.

The kettle boiled and switched itself off. He poured some water into the cup.

JAZMIN HEARD HER MUM'S KEY IN THE DOOR. SHE GOT UP FROM HER BED AND WENT OUT ONTO THE LANDING. SHE LOOKED DOWN. SOMETHING ABOUT THE RIGID SET OF HER MUM'S SHOULDERS AS she shrugged off her coat suggested that maybe she wasn't the only one who'd had a difficult time. The old man had been stalling again, she thought. Playing his waiting game. She guessed that her mum'd had another fruitless session. She scooted downstairs.

"Hi. Want a cup of coffee? Shall I make it for you?" she suggested.

Assia smiled, nodded distractedly. "That'd be nice, hon," she sighed. "Have you had any lunch?"

"Lots," Jazmin lied. In reality, she'd been too upset by the constant stream of nasty text messages to eat. It seemed like suddenly everybody in the whole world knew what she'd been up to. Her life had turned into a bad TV soap. It was really scary. Now she led the way to the kitchen, grateful for something to do to distract herself.

"Everything all right?" she asked as she found her mum's favourite mug.

There was a pause.

"Mmm," Assia said distantly, resting her elbows on the table and staring at nothing.

Jazmin filled the cafetière.

The pause turned into a silence.

Fine, Jazmin thought to herself. If her mum didn't want to talk about her day, that was absolutely fine. She didn't want to talk about her day either.

FIRST THING MONDAY MORNING, ASSIA HUSTLED INTO HER BOSS'S OFFICE WITHOUT KNOCKING AND WITHOUT EVEN STOPPING OFF AT HER DESK TO UNLOAD HER STUFF FIRST.

"I need to talk to you, sir," she said abruptly, closing the outer door behind her.

"Uh-huh." The head of the ISA was sorting through a large folder. "You know, we really need to get rid of this cold-case file," he remarked with a sigh. "Some of these unsolved assignments have been hanging around for ages." He glanced up at Assia, noticed for the first time the tense expression on her face. He closed the folder, and gestured her towards a seat.

Assia sat down. The head of the ISA swivelled his chair round to face her. "It's Kirilovitch, isn't it? You've got something important out of him at last."

Assia nodded. "He confessed to me yesterday that he did know about the organ trafficking."

"See – what did I tell you! He was there, he had to know what was going on."

"But there's more..."

The head of the ISA leaned his chin upon his hands and regarded her steadily. "Go on," he said evenly.

Assia paused. She had thought long and hard about how to communicate to her boss what Kirilovitch had revealed to her. In the end, she'd decided to tell him the story exactly as the old man had told her. So Assia described how Kirilovitch had returned to the Arkadia Clinic late one night to retrieve some patient records he needed to update. How he pulled into the car park, and saw two of the biggest, blackest Mercedes he had ever seen waiting off to one side.

Curious, he had parked his car and got out. Some instinct had told him to avoid the main entrance, even though one of the heavy glass doors had been left temptingly half-open. Instead, he walked quietly and cautiously to the back of the clinic, to where the nursing and auxiliary staff had their own separate entrance. Entering the building via the deserted kitchen quarters, he had made his way along the darkened corridors until he reached the main operating theatre.

The old man had told Assia how he saw a strip of light under the operating theatre door, how he had entered the sluice room, and peered through one of the porthole windows. And what he had seen was his father-in-law, Boris Arkady, in full medical scrubs, surrounded by a small medical team whose names and faces he did not know.

Arkady was bent over the operating table, performing some sort of operation. Kirilovitch could not see exactly what was going on, but from the position of the surgeon, and the support team, he deduced that the patient was undergoing some sort of invasive cranio-facial surgery, although he could not recall anybody currently at the clinic who was, or who would ever be booked in for such a procedure. Kirilovitch stood in the dim light of the icy-cold sluice room, and watched what was happening in frozen fascination.

RECONSTRUCTIVE SURGERY WAS NOT NEW. IN 1994, A NINE-YEAR-OLD CHILD IN NORTHERN INDIA LOST HER FACE AND SCALP IN A THRESHING MACHINE ACCIDENT. SURGEONS WERE ABLE TO reconnect the arteries and replant the skin. Since then, fingers, hands, thighs, arms and legs had all been reattached, using microsurgery. But face to face transplants had taken time to become established, not just because of the moral and ethical ambiguities surrounding the procedure, or the reluctance of people to donate their faces when they died, even though they were constantly assured that the transplanted face would look different on the new owner. The problem was that the operation was extraordinarily complex and fraught with difficulty.

It involved firstly "degloving" the donor's face from the corpse. Then the skin, facial muscles and subcutaneous fat was removed from the recipient's face, after which the donor's face with its lips, chin, nose and eight major blood vessels had to be grafted into place. Essential to the transplant's success was the need to encourage the regeneration of the cut facial nerves, which meant the extensive application of growth factors and immunosuppressants. The biggest post-operative problem surgeons always faced was creating tolerance within the patient's system, because skin produced a stronger immune reaction than any other organ in the body. Only with the recent dramatic developments in specialist drugs and nano-surgical techniques could surgeons attempt full face to face transplants with confidence.

MEDICAL ETIQUETTE FORBADE KIRILOVITCH FROM ENTERING THE OPERATING THEATRE – IT WAS NOT, AFTER ALL, HIS PATIENT, AND HE WAS WEARING ORDINARY STREET CLOTHES. SO, STUNNED BY what he had witnessed, he had merely retrieved the files he needed, then gone back to his car. However, he secretly determined to return to the clinic early next day to check up on the mystery patient.

The following morning, Kirilovitch had arrived at the clinic to find the two Mercedes had gone. Entering by the front door this time, he greeted the receptionist and asked to see the patient lists and the overnight notes. There was no record of any facial operation having taken place the night before. No post-operative reports. He checked all the rooms. No new patients had been admitted.

The mystery was deepening.

Kirilovitch had told Assia that he was now faced with a dilemma. What he wanted to do was ask Arkady for an explanation of what he had stumbled upon the previous night. But their relationship was not easy. Since his marriage to Anna, it had deteriorated markedly. Once he was "our brilliant new doctor from Moscow". Now, Boris Arkady treated him with a frosty, distant courtesy. The way Kirilovitch rationalized it, he had stolen from the great surgeon one of his prize possessions: his beautiful daughter.

So he did not feel he could broach the subject with Arkady. But there was another avenue to explore. Arkady was fanatical about keeping records – you had to be in a business where suing was all too easy for rich clients with sharp lawyers. Thus every appointment, every procedure was always logged, so that the clinic could not be blamed for any perceived failure on its part. Somewhere, Kirilovitch knew, there would be a full account of the operation that had taken place. If it was not on the clinic computer it would be on Arkady's personal one. All he had to do was break into and scan his father-in-law's private computer. But to do that, he'd have to return to the clinic at a time when Boris Arkady was not there, and enter his office, his private sanctum.

"Which was exactly what he did," Assia said. "And a couple of days later, Kirilovitch discovered what Boris Arkady had secretly been up to."

The head of the ISA leaned forward in his chair, his chin resting on his hands, his eyes narrowed and focused. "Go on," he said quietly.

"Kirilovitch 'borrowed' Arkady's personal number to access the data," Assia said. "And it was all there, meticulously recorded, just as he knew it would be. The man's name, last location, before and after facial images – together with a full list of surgical procedures, the patient's blood type, and his DNA profile. Kirilovitch says your DNA is practically the only thing that can't be surgically altered. And as he suspected, the mystery patient had undergone a total face transplant."

The head of the ISA uttered a startled exclamation. He stared incredulously at her.

"There's more. Kirilovitch recognized him," Assia went on. "The man whose face appeared on the screen was the leader of the region's Mafia. He was wanted by the police for years of violent drug-related murders. His picture had been on the TV news, in all the papers."

"And Arkady had given him a new identity?"

Assia nodded. "Exactly. Now, nobody would recognize him again. Once the scars had healed, he could walk down any street anywhere in the world in total safety. It was the ultimate and foolproof disguise. But he wasn't the only one. As Kirilovitch scrolled through the file, he came across other individuals whose faces had also been changed. People from all over the world had come to the clinic secretly to have their identity obliterated, and a new one created surgically for them by Boris Arkady.

"Obviously Kirilovitch didn't know who they all were, but he could make an educated guess. You didn't have to be a genius to work out why somebody would choose to undergo something so drastic and invasive as face transplant surgery."

Assia paused. The head of the ISA went on staring at her in silence.

"Another thing Kirilovitch said he noticed was that the donor faces were all very much younger than the recipients," she went on. "They appeared to come from people in their twenties and thirties."

There was another pause while the head of the ISA absorbed this new revelation.

"So it looks as if along with the organ trafficking, Boris Arkady was up to something far more serious than even we suspected," Assia concluded.

The head of the ISA frowned. "I don't understand it," he said slowly. "Our Russian colleagues Miusov and Korolenko went through that clinic and all its computers with a fine toothcomb. If this file existed how come they didn't find it?"

Assia did a palms-up. "I guess that Arkady has deleted

the original document. Or hidden it somewhere safe."

In the long silence that followed, Assia could see from her boss's expression that he was struggling to come to terms with the horrific implications of what she had just told him. Exactly as she had done when the old man had shared his ghastly secret with her.

"You really believe Kirilovitch is telling us the truth?" the head of the ISA asked finally.

Assia nodded. "Yes I do," she declared firmly.

"And he has a copy of the file with him?"

"He told me he has."

There was a brief silence.

The head of the ISA's features untensed fractionally. "Well. Who would have thought the poor old man would turn out to be so useful after all. Of course he's agreed to give you the copy?"

Assia let a split second pass before replying. "No," she said bluntly.

"Excuse me?"

"Kirilovitch has come up with some conditions. Before he'll hand over the file to us, we have to find his wife and daughter for him. And he wants a written undertaking to say we'll do it. If we don't agree, he won't give us the file. If we can't find them, he won't give us the file, and he won't testify at Arkady's trial either." Assia shrugged, pulling a rueful face. "I'm afraid he's not quite the poor old man we thought he was," she observed drily.

WHILE ASSIA WAS REPORTING BACK TO HER BOSS, JAZMIN WAS TRYING HARD TO DEVELOP AN ILLNESS. THE SORT OF ILLNESS THAT MEANT YOU HAD TO TURN AROUND AND GO STRAIGHT BACK HOME. The sort that involved hiding under the duvet with lots of hot chocolate and TV. Trouble was, although her mind was working hard, coming up with a whole bunch of symptoms, her body was refusing to produce them at short notice.

Taking as much time as she could, and walking so slowly she was practically going backwards, Jazmin idled along the pavement until she reached the learning centre gate, where the usual crowd of female clone rangers were hanging about, spreading their own brand of negative charisma.

As soon as she saw them, Jazmin pulled the collar of her jacket up to her ears and wound her woolly scarf around her face. Pre-emptive camouflage. She quickened her pace. Maybe she was going to get by unnoticed. As if. The instant she drew level with them, the whole group went into a huddle. Then they separated out and stood in a line either side of the gate, like a guard of honour at a wedding. They began whistling. At first, she wasn't sure what they were whistling because she didn't instantly recognize the tune. Then she realized: it was the "Hi ho" song from *Snow White*.

Hahaha, very funny, Jazmin thought grimly, sticking her chin defiantly into the air. She walked through the group, blanking them. She'd nearly reached the safety of the front steps when Fion, whose big grin clearly said it was payback time, called out loudly, "Oh look girls, there goes one of the seven dwarves! Which one is it, I wonder? Could it be Happy?"

"Nooooo," chorused the whistlers. They'd obviously rehearsed this.

"Could it be Bashful?" Fion asked.

"Noooo."

"Doc?"

"Noooo."

"Well then, it must be Sleepy!"

All the girls burst out laughing. Jazmin felt her cheeks going bright red with embarrassment. She stared straight ahead, doing her level best to ignore them.

"Of course, it might be Dopey," some joker in the crowd suggested.

Shoulders rigid with held-in anger, Jazmin shoved a couple of younger students rudely aside and stalked up the steps. Gritting her teeth and grim-faced, she headed for the main building. Other students stopped what they were doing, and turned to watch her. Behind her back, the mocking whistling started up again. It followed her all the way to the door.

Eventually, she would look back on all this and laugh, Jazmin thought to herself darkly as she hustled through the glass double doors, and almost fell over Honi Delacy and Zeb Stone, who were standing right in the entrance, poring over an open textbook, their heads close together. Zeb was carefully explaining something to Honi in his usual earnest tone of voice. Honi was gazing at him, worshipful and wide-eyed, nodding every couple of seconds, as if she understood what he was saying, which Jazmin was pretty sure she did not.

Jazmin tried to creep around them, but Honi had obviously set this up, and had been waiting some time for Jazmin to arrive. Pretending to be absorbed in the book, she "accidentally" bumped into Jazmin. Jazmin glared. Honi flashed her a triumphant, gloating grin, which she followed with a jaunty little finger wave. Zeb was so absorbed in the textbook that he didn't even look up and see her. Jazmin gave Honi a look as wooden as a furniture warehouse. Some day soon she would get her revenge upon Honi Delacy, she promised herself as she made her way to her locker. And it would be revenge so sweet, you could ice a cake with it.

NIKOLAI ARKADY, SON OF BORIS ARKADY, LIKED USING THE UNDERGROUND SYSTEM TO GET AROUND LONDON. IT WAS QUICKER AND CHEAPER THAN TAKING A TAXI, AND HAVING LIVED IN MOSCOW for most of his adult life he was, like most Muscovites, used to travelling everywhere by Metro.

Not that any of the London underground stations could

match the magnificent splendour of the Komsomolskaya, with its chandeliers and gold-encrusted mosaics. Or the marble and stainless steel elegance of the Mayakovskaya. He sat back in his seat and surveyed his fellow passengers with a feeling of benign tolerance. It was Monday morning. He had had a good breakfast at his exclusive Mayfair hotel, and now he was on his way to Canary Wharf for a business meeting.

Nikolai enjoyed doing business in Britain. Compared to his home country, it was so much easier. In Russia, you needed documents to do anything. And each one had to be obtained by bribing some sharp-faced official who wanted his back-hander before he'd move a centimetre from his desk. Over there, it was a shark pool. Over here, however, it was like a stroll through a kiddies' playground. All he had to remember to do was flatter and be charming, and the doors flew open for him. It was like his father always said: with the American and the Brit, you watch your mouth; with the Italian, your back and with the Russian, you watch your wallet.

Nikolai Arkady picked up a local newspaper discarded by someone who'd just left the carriage, and began flicking idly through its pages, until his attention was suddenly caught by a photograph of a young boy and a much older man sitting opposite each other at a table, a chessboard between them. Their heads were bent over the board; they were wholly absorbed in the game.

Arkady's dark, watchful eyes narrowed as he looked down at the photo. He opened his organizer, got out a small picture and compared it with the picture in the paper. Then he carefully read the accompanying article, which was headlined: *Chess Mates – players battle it out at Saturday's major London chess competition!* He continued reading without looking up until the train reached his stop. Every now and then, he marked something in the story with his silver pen. Finally he left the carriage, taking the newspaper with him.

THE SENIOR LIBRARIAN MANNING THE ENQUIRIES DESK SIGHED AS HE PICKED UP THE PHONE. IT HAD BEEN ONE OF THOSE MORNINGS. STUPID READERS LINING UP WITH THEIR STUPID QUESTIONS. IN HIS opinion, libraries would be much better places if members of the public were kept out of them. They only made a mess of his perfectly ordered shelves and wasted his time. He had a pile of paperwork to do, and three of his junior staff had phoned in sick (given that it was Monday, they were probably hungover, he thought in disgust). Which meant he was going to have to work through his lunch break. Now there was another potential time-waster on the end of the phone.

"Yes?" he barked crisply into the mouthpiece.

The man at the other end was polite, precise. He quite understood that the librarian was a busy man, he said, but he had a problem. It was his son, he explained. He had taken part in the chess match at the weekend – perhaps the librarian had seen his picture in the paper? Anyway, the silly boy had left his brand-new sports bag in the hall. Had it been handed in at all? The librarian was able to assure him positively that it had not been.

Well then, the man continued smoothly, probably somebody had picked it up on the day and handed it to one of the organizers. He would really appreciate it if the librarian could give him a name and a number to contact – his son had lost the details; you know what boys are like!

Wearily, the librarian punched up the details of the competition on his screen and gave a contact number to the man at the other end of the phone. Grateful thanks were proffered. Then the man rang off, and the librarian went to investigate a group of truanting teenage boys who were thumbing through a textbook on anatomy and sniggering.

A SHORT WHILE LATER, JAZMIN WAS SITTING AT THE BACK OF THE MATHS CLASS TRYING HER VERY BEST TO BLEND WITH THE SCENERY. DESPITE WHAT HER *EX*-FRIEND ZEB THOUGHT, SHE actually hated maths; it was her worst subject, and the class facilitator, a tall, sarcastic woman in her mid-thirties, hated her. Taken all together, it was a scenario made in hell.

Jazmin stared listlessly at her textbook, where sets of incomprehensible equations marched relentlessly across the page. Why did she have to learn this? she wondered. What was the point? Just how often in the future was she really going to *need* it?

Picking up her pen, Jazmin started work on the equations. She filled in all the noughts and turned the ones into little dancing men. She was just about to make unicycles out of the fives, when she suddenly became aware that the drony voice at the front of the room had stopped. She looked up. The facilitator was regarding her balefully, with her arms folded. The traditional sarky adult stance. The rest of the class had also turned round and were eyeing Jazmin with bright-eyed and excited expectation. The traditional stance of spectators at a public hanging. Yikes.

"Jazmin Dawson," the facilitator said softly in a voice that had claws in it.

Jazmin hastily assumed a keen and innocently helpful expression. "Yes?"

"Perhaps you'd like to help us out here. If it's not too much trouble?"

"Unh?" Jazmin looked around for help; she found none.

"The problem on the board," the facilitator continued silkily. "Would you care to solve it for us?"

Jazmin stared at the board. It was full of little xs and ys and complicated patterns of brackets. She hadn't a clue what to do.

"Oh. Well. I..."

"We talked about this last week, Jazmin," the facilitator said drily. "I assumed you were paying attention. Your eyes *were* open, as I recall. Your head *was* up off the desk."

To the accompaniment of sniggering and whispered comments, Jazmin stood up and made her way slowly to the front of the room. Her face was flaming. She picked up the board marker and looked at the problem, wondering if some higher power might make the marker suddenly melt in her hand, or the board fall on her head and knock her unconscious. When neither of those things happened she scribbled a few tentative numbers and tried to ignore the rising tide of laughter behind her back.

A long, long time seemed to pass.

Then: "Sit down, Jazmin," the facilitator said wearily.

Jazmin embarked upon the Walk of Shame.

"Would anybody else like to show Jazmin how to solve the equation?" the facilitator asked in an exaggeratedly pained voice.

Almost at once, Honi's hand shot up into the air. Without waiting to be invited, she rose gracefully to her feet, and strode quickly out to the front, shooting Jazmin a pitying glance as they passed each other midway. Honi picked up the marker, considered the problem for a moment, head on one side, hand on hip. Then she began working her way neatly and methodically through it.

Meanwhile Jazmin made her way back to her desk. She slid into her seat, keeping her head down and her eyes lowered. This was gruesome to the amount of ten. Jaz Dawson, ace crime fighter and secret agent, would never have let herself be humiliated by Honi Delacy, a girl who couldn't even add up her paycard bill without counting on her fingers, she thought disgustedly. Unh, mental head slap. It was so embarrassing.

IVAN KIRILOVITCH STOOD IN HIS KITCHEN, HELPING HIMSELF TO ANOTHER MILK CHOCOLATE DIGESTIVE BISCUIT. THE BISCUITS IN ENGLAND WERE VERY GOOD, HE THOUGHT. AND THERE WERE SO many varieties to choose from too. So far he had sampled Highland shortbread, ginger nuts, bourbons and custard creams.

The old man crunched his biscuit and checked the time: Assia would be here soon. He wondered how she had got on in her meeting with her boss. He smiled wryly. He was prepared to bet that her boss would not like what she had had to tell. Tough. He wasn't going to change his mind. He suspected that if he gave them the file now, he would become redundant. They wouldn't need him any more, and they would have no incentive to look for his wife and daughter. He liked Assia, and he was sorry to do this to her, but he knew how these people worked.

It was better this way, he thought, as he moved the rest of the biscuits around so that it didn't look like any had been eaten. Better for him, at any rate. If they did what he wanted, then he would do what they wanted. A win-win scenario. And maybe then, if it all worked out, he would finally be able to make peace with the past, and go home.

Home. The word snagged him like a briar stem. The old guy paused, one hand hovering over the plate. He looked up and stared straight ahead. Straight through the wall, and straight into the past. Grief at what he had lost and regret at what he had failed to do suddenly caught him unawares. He felt hollowed, a great emptiness in the pit of his stomach. Then he heard footsteps on the gravel path outside. He forced himself to return to the present. Uttering a sigh, he went to the door to let Assia in, and find out what she had to say to him.

AS SOON AS THE BELL WENT FOR THE END OF CLASS, JAZMIN SLOWLY PACKED AWAY HER BOOKS. STILL KEEPING HER HEAD DOWN, AND AVOIDING ANY EYE CONTACT, SHE WAITED UNTIL THE room had almost emptied and the last few students had got up to go. Then she scuttled out of the room in their wake.

And ran straight into Honi and her friends, who were waiting for her in the corridor.

Jazmin decided to ignore the bullies completely this time. She'd endured enough grief already. She edged past, pretending to be searching for something in her bag.

As if it could ever be that easy!

"Hey, Jazmin! Wait up!" Honi commanded.

Jazmin feigned deafness and went on walking.

Honi moved fast. She zipped along the corridor and placed herself directly in front of Jazmin. Jazmin halted. She had no choice. She sighed deeply, eye-rolled and slapped a disdainful "Yeah – so?" expression onto her face.

"Aw, what's up?" Honi teased. "Couldn't Jazmin solve the BIG maths problem? Was it too BIG for you?" she scoffed.

"That's heightist!" Jazmin snapped back.

"Heightist?" Honi sniggered. "I don't think so!" She blinked, took a step back and surveyed Jazmin slowly from top to toe. Grinning, she leaned forward and pointed at her hair. "So tell me, what is this – a hairdo or a hairdon't?" she observed.

Jazmin felt her cheeks flooding with colour. "Excuse me?"

"Ugh, and as for those *clothes*," Honi went on. "I mean they're like, totally charity shop. Jazmin, hasn't anybody told you the bag-lady look is *sooo* ageing?"

The girls in the background exchanged delighted glances and giggled.

Jazmin mentally checked out Honi's current outfit

which consisted of white kilted skirt and fluffy pink jumper. "Better than looking like a refugee from Mothercare," she snapped back, with a facial expression that could have hammered rivets.

"At least I have style," Honi told her loftily.

"Yeah? At least I know lipgloss isn't one of the four major food groups," Jazmin responded.

Sensing a fight developing, Honi grinned delightedly. "Oooh, getting snippy! Just because a certain new boy prefers me to you. Hey, I wonder which one of us has a *date* tonight? Could it be you? No, I don't think so! Oh – then it must be me!"

Honi cut Jazmin a pitying glance. Then, before her victim could access her mental Withering Things To Say File, she gathered her gang together, and they all sauntered off in the direction of the canteen, laughing.

Jazmin sucked in some air. Time for a reality check, she thought. Before she went down with severe Loss of Perspective syndrome. She reminded herself firmly that this was *Honi Delacy* she was mad with. A girl who had to shop once a day to stop herself developing mallorexia, and the sole reason she'd been able to solve that maths problem in class was not because she was a hidden genius, but because she'd somehow managed to lock down her one brain cell long enough to take in what Zeb had told her earlier. Deep down, she was really shallow.

However.

Jazmin did a face scrunch. She did not like admitting it, even to herself, but Honi's nasty jibes about her clothes had actually hit home. How dare Honi imply that she didn't have any style? She had loads of style, she thought indignantly. Style ran in her family. She surveyed her washed-out jeans, baggy at the knee and fraying at the hem, and topped today by a long-sleeved grey Gap T. Hadn't Honi heard of vintage? Unh.

So maybe today was not one of her stylishly best days, Jazmin decided, but some days she dressed head to toe designer. There were all the stretchy figure-enhancing outfits and leather belts with studs and designer heels she wore... Well, okay maybe *she* didn't, but her drop-dead gorgeous alter-ego did, which was near enough.

Slapping a stiff-upper-lippy expression onto her face, Jazmin shouldered her bag and followed Honi and Delta and the rest of her class in the direction of the canteen. It was breaktime and she was in bad need of some calorific comfort. Barging through the double doors, she attached herself to the queue at the hatch. When her turn came, she selected lasagne, a piece of chocolate cake and some pineapple juice. Then, muttering darkly under her breath, she carried her tray to a table on the far side of the room. Okay, maybe she was acting like a stupid idiot, she admitted. But at least she was a stupid idiot with food.

THE CONFIDENT YOUNG CROUPIER AT THE RITZ CLUB CASINO WAS PERFECTLY ACCUSTOMED TO DEALING WITH THE SORT OF RICH FOREIGN TOURIST WHO LIKED NOTHING BETTER THAN WHILING AWAY their afternoon at the gaming tables. Even so, the dark-haired Russian businessman leaning with casual nonchalance at the far end of the table was creeping her out with his smile. She was trying to look away, but the smile kept dragging her back. It was a smile with an agenda. A smile you wanted to back away from fast.

"Place your bets, gentlemen," she announced nervously, smoothing down her blonde hair and forcing herself to concentrate once more upon the roulette wheel. The dark-haired Russian immediately gathered up his pile of gambling chips, and moved them deliberately into the centre of the table. "Everything on red," he said softly. The croupier paused, waiting until the other players had made their bets. "All done, gentlemen?" she asked, then tossed in the ball and spun the wheel.

The croupier focused her gaze on the spinning wheel. Red and black squares turned into red and black snakes as it spun faster and faster. The small crowd of players round the table waited expectantly. The wheel slowed, the ball rattling bonily from side to side like a tiny skull, until it finally came to rest. "Red wins," the croupier announced. There was a gasp from the assembled punters. They all turned to stare at the Russian businessman.

"Hey, you played well today, my friend," one of the gamblers remarked enviously.

The Russian shrugged. He leaned forward to gather up the chips. "A game is only worth playing if you win," he said coolly, shooting his cuffs to reveal a set of sparkling gold and diamond cufflinks. He picked up his chips, once more smiling the smile that had so unnerved the croupier. "And whatever the game, sooner or later I always win," he added.

KIRILOVITCH OPENED THE FRONT DOOR. ASSIA GREETED HIM, AND WALKED BRISKLY INTO THE LIVING ROOM. "THE ISA WILL AGREE TO WHAT YOU WANT," SHE TOLD HIM.

The old man bent his head in acknowledgement, silently noting that Assia had said "The ISA", making it impersonal, keeping herself out of the picture, as if their relationship was something separate. A line had been drawn. He liked the way she did that.

Assia withdrew a slim document file from her briefcase and handed it to him. "This is the written agreement. It's been signed by my boss, the head of the ISA in London."

He took the file, skimmed the contents, nodded, and set it down on the coffee table.

"Please sit," he said, indicating a chair. Assia sat down. She waited while he limped into the kitchen, returning shortly with two mugs of strong black tea and the plate of biscuits. By some mutually unspoken agreement, the conversation turned to ordinary subjects for a while. Safe topics like the weather, the cat, Jazmin's latest exploits. Then Assia picked up her mug and stared down into the half-drunk dark liquid. "May I ask you something?" she said.

"Go ahead."

"What happened to you after you'd copied Boris Arkady's secret file?"

There was a long silence. Eventually, just as Assia was about to apologize for intruding upon what were personal, and clearly still painful events, Kirilovitch spoke: "He knew that I'd been there, that night. One of the Mercedes drivers had tipped him off," he said quietly. "He guessed that eventually I would come back, that I would not be able to resist the overwhelming desire to find out the truth. So when I finally made the decision to search, he was waiting for me in the darkness."

"But he didn't stop you?"

"Oh no. That was the arrogance of the man. In his eyes, I was nothing. He wouldn't lower himself to quarrel with me. He didn't have to. He had a far more cunning and effective way of ensuring my silence: my wife and my daughter."

The old man's mouth tightened into a grim line. "The next day, Boris Arkady called me into his office. He told me, in that precise, cold way he had, that if I ever told anybody what I had discovered, he would deny it. And if the file ever came to light in the future, if I tried to discredit him in any way, he would make sure that I never saw my wife and child again." Kirilovitch shivered. "I knew he meant it too. Boris Arkady was completely ruthless. There was nothing he wouldn't do to preserve his reputation."

Assia shook her head sympathetically. "It must have been an impossible situation for you."

"It was like walking on quicksand. I was perpetually on edge, wondering what he was going to do next. Every day, I could feel the tension building. I sensed he was waiting, like a cat watching shadows. Of course my wife noticed the change in me too – she kept asking what was the matter. I could not tell her. We had always shared everything before, and it tore me up inside, not being able to confide in her. She loved her father so much you see, she venerated him. I couldn't destroy that for her.

"Then one day, a week after our encounter in the dark, Arkady summoned me to his office. He told me he had arranged for me to represent him at a big medical conference in New York. It was all planned out. The flight was booked, hotel sorted. I was to leave the following evening. Immediately I was suspicious – what was he planning to do with Natacha and Anna while I was gone? What lies was he going to tell them about me?

"I did not want to leave, but I had no choice. And he knew it." Kirilovitch's eyes misted over with memory.

"I remember packing my case for the trip. Saying goodbye to Anna. Promising to bring Natacha back something wonderful from America.

"I was just loading up the car, when Anna came running out of the house, shouting that her father had called, there was an important document I needed, I must drive quickly to the clinic and collect it. I was already running late, so I drove as fast as the icy roads would permit. And then it happened: I was passing through the forest, when my brakes failed and the car crashed.

"It was as I was crawling from the wreckage, bleeding and covered in shards of glass that the realization finally dawned. This was what Arkady had been planning. He wanted to get rid of me, and this was the way it was meant to happen – a fake 'accident'. Suddenly, everything slotted into place. It made perfect sense. If I died, nobody would ever find out what he had been doing. He kept hold of his secret, and his daughter and granddaughter too."

Kirilovitch continued: "I was so scared – mainly that Arkady might find out I hadn't died in the accident and send one of his associates to come and finish me off. My instinct was to get as far from the area as I could. So I decided to walk to Perm, the nearest big town, even though it was freezing cold, and I wasn't dressed for the outdoors. It was a totally stupid thing to do, but looking back, I must have been suffering from concussion – I wasn't thinking straight.

"When I eventually got to Perm a day later, I discovered that my 'death' was already in the papers, and on the local news. Arkady hadn't wasted any time! I sat in a cheap hotel room and watched the reports about myself on TV. I saw pictures of the burned-out car; I saw Boris Arkady talking to reporters about how it was a terrible tragedy, what a fine doctor I had been. It was all so strange. So surreal."

The old man paused, glanced away. "I saw my wife and daughter dressed in black, their faces pale, being led away from the forest. It cracked open my heart! She looked so beautiful, my wife, Anna. In her long velvet cape with the fur collar. I'd bought it for her in Moscow, in one of the stylish shops along the Kuznetsky Most." He smiled sadly. "At least her tears were real." Kirilovitch was silent for a few moments. He always found that image of his wife and child walking away so unbearably painful, that every time he remembered it, he had to stop, to replace the mental picture with another one; the image of a future where his wife and child were running towards him, their eyes alight with love and welcome. Then he went on: "Oh yes, Boris Arkady had it all under control," he said. "You couldn't fault him. One night, I sat in my hotel room, and watched a retrospective programme all about my life. It had interviews with patients I had treated successfully, comments from the nursing staff. Arkady wanted everyone to knew that I was well and truly liked, but well and truly dead. It was an excellent piece of invention. After a while I almost began to believe it myself! Except that every time I looked in the bathroom mirror, and saw my swollen, almost unrecognizable face, I knew that I was Ivan Kirilovitch, and that unbelievable as it might seem I was still very much alive."

"And then?"

"For a while, I actually thought I might go to the Perm police, and say to them: 'Look, here I am. It's a miracle – I didn't die after all!' But I knew that if I tried, Arkady would only arrange another 'accident'. Sooner or later. I had discovered his secret. I was a threat. The only thing I knew for sure was that I could never return to my old life. Ironically, Arkady was right: I was to all intents and purposes, a 'dead' man."

Assia cradled her mug between her hands. She regarded Kirilovitch steadily. "So what did you decide to do?" she asked him.

"I stayed in Perm for nearly a week, keeping to my room as much as possible, until I had recovered enough to contemplate making a move," the old man said. "And then, I caught the train to Moscow. For a while, I stayed in my family's *dacha*, deep in the forest outside the city. My parents were dead, but we still owned the land and the house," he gestured towards the bedroom, "that's where the icons come from," he added. "Then I went north to the port city of Arkhangelsk. It was thousands of miles away, right on the other side of the country. A place where nobody would recognize me.

"I had been stationed there for a bit when I was in the army, so I knew my way around. The city was snowbound from the end of October until the beginning of April, but I reckoned I would be just in time to pick up a ship. They always needed guys on the big ships. And they were reputed to be not too fussy about papers and things like that."

The old guy stared into his mug, as if reading his past in the leaves.

"I reached Arkhangelsk the second week in October," he said, "it was an unpleasant place. Dirty, and freezing cold. Sky smoky from factories. The river Dvina yellow with chemicals. When you breathed in, the air caught the back of your throat and made it sting. I remember seeing a line of barges, black against the grey sky, all chained together like convicts, chugging north towards the White Sea, and there were packs of stray dogs scavenging for food amongst the trash piled up on the windswept pavement. Like things from another century. It was a place that had given up on itself. A dump.

"As soon as I arrived, I made my way to the dock area and there was a café. There always is. A typical old-style *stolovaya*, a self-service place. I had forgotten what they were like. Bare tabletops, the floor wet with melted snow. Fug of tobacco and damp clothing. Shabby people eyeing you suspiciously. I ordered some food: a bowl of cabbage soup, some black bread and coffee, and I sat and nursed them all morning.

"After that, I went and inquired about work at the harbour master's office. He informed me there was a freighter due in a week, so I found a cheap place to stay and waited out the days until it arrived. It was the loneliest time of my life. I walked the cold streets, sat in the gloomy free library and read. I ate as cheaply as I could and tried to come to terms with the fact that from now on I was utterly alone in the world. When I boarded that ship, I was Ivan Kirilovitch, a Russian doctor with a wife and child somewhere in the east. Three years later, when I left it, I was Jean Brun, a simple French sailor. A nobody with nothing."

Assia said: "And you never ever tried to make contact with your family in all that time? I find that so incredibly hard to understand."

The old man smiled thinly. "Dead men don't call," he said wearily.

"But—"

"No," he cut across her words. "Believe me, I turned it over and over in my mind. Worked through every conceivable scenario. Every time I saw myself walking through my front door, my wife and daughter's face lighting up with joy, I thought: 'And then? Where would we go? How would we live? No place in the world would ever be home for us.'

"I knew Arkady had contacts all over the globe. People who owed him their lives. Other people who'd do anything to stop him revealing their true identity. Gratitude or fear. One way or another, he would find somebody to track us down. So it was better that my family forgot me. Better and safer for all of us."

Assia bent her head in acknowledgement. "I understand," she said quietly. "And then you moved to Paris?"

The old man nodded. "It was where Anna and I went on honeymoon," he said simply. "Our special city. I thought I could still feel close to her if I lived there. I used to imagine that maybe I'd walk round a corner one day, and suddenly, there she'd be. I did a bunch of jobs to support myself – hospital porter, night security guard, that sort of thing. Sold an icon whenever hunger came knocking." He glanced at her. "And now you know everything about me," he said.

Assia glanced at him. She saw how pale his face had become, the lines of weariness etched on his face. He looked absolutely drained.

"Thank you for sharing that," she said quietly. She stood up, collected the tea things and carried them to the kitchen. Then she came back into the living room. "Is there anything else I can do for you before I go?" she asked gently.

"No thank you. You're very kind," the old man

murmured, but Assia knew that he was barely aware of her presence. His mind was elsewhere, travelling along the newly remembered paths from the past. She slipped on her coat, and let herself quietly out of the house.

THE END OF THE AFTERNOON FOUND JAZMIN BACK IN HER ROOM, STARING MOODILY OUT OF THE WINDOW. SHEESH, WHAT AN AWFUL DAY. OPENING HER GEOGRAPHY TEXTBOOK, SHE TRIED TO rationalize what was going on with her life right now. Perhaps this was some sort of pre-emptive karma, she thought. She was getting all the bad stuff over with before the good stuff started happening. On the other hand, maybe it wasn't. In which case, maybe she ought to consider other life choices.

Like emigrating.

Jazmin flicked through the pages of the textbook. Australia looked good: the climate was nice and hot, and the daily food consumption seemed to be high. And it had the great advantage of being on the other side of the world. Honi and her mates couldn't laugh at her, bully her or humiliate her. She sighed wearily and began to fill in her homework chart.

Jazmin worked on steadily until it began to get dark outside. She only realized she was no longer alone when she looked up and saw her mother standing in the doorway, arms folded, steadily watching her. She was not smiling. Uh-oh, Jazmin thought. Not *again*! She ran a quick mental check. No major crimes came to mind.

"Um...hi, Mum," she said brightly. "Nice day?"

Her mum bypassed the friendly greeting. "Do you know where I've just been?" she remarked, her voice steely.

"To see the Russian guy? Hey, how was he...?" Jazmin's voice tailed off as she caught the frosty expression in her mum's eye.

"Yes, actually I did call in on him this afternoon. And thank you, he is fine. But *after* that, I went to your learning centre, to see your head of year. In response to the urgent phone call I had at work when I got back to the office."

"Oh," Jazmin said in a small voice. So that was what this was all about. Darn!

"Yes, 'Oh' is about right. Honestly, Jazmin, what were you thinking of?"

"Err...I..."

"Homework not being handed in! Deadlines missed! Did you think I wouldn't find out?"

Yes, Jazmin thought. *Believe it or not, that's exactly what I thought. Guess I was wrong.*

"And what about the letters?" her mum asked sternly.

"Letters?"

"The school sent two letters. What happened to them?"

Jazmin assumed a look of innocent bewilderment. "I don't know. I'm sure I put a letter in the kitchen some time ago. Didn't you get it?"

"Strangely enough, no."

"Ah. Sorry. Maybe it fell down behind one of the units?"

Assia smiled thinly. "Oh really? Well, I never thought of that. And the other letter?"

"Must be lost in the post?" Jazmin suggested.

There was a long pause.

Assia sighed deeply. "It's just not good enough, is it?"

"Uh. No," Jazmin agreed meekly, bowing her head. She had learned over the years that the quickest way to get her mum off her back was to agree with everything she said. It made her clockwork run down quicker.

"You're not a child any more, are you?"

"No."

"I thought I could rely on you."

"You can."

"So what are you going to do about it?"

"Work harder?" Jazmin suggested. She gesticulated with one hand at her desk. "Look, see, I am actually doing my homework."

"Hmmm. Well, I suppose that's a start. Because things certainly need to change."

"Oh they will, I promise you," Jazmin agreed earnestly. "Hey, I'm not moving from this desk until I've finished."

Assia gave her a long, silent and searching look. Then, clamping her lips together into a thin line, she turned and went, shutting the door behind her.

Jazmin stared at the closed door. Australia it was then, she told herself grimly. It was either that, or a one-way ticket to therapy-land.

IT WAS 5.30 A.M. THE TiME WHEN SLEEP REACHES iTS LOWEST LEVEL; WHEN THE CURVE OF THE REM CYCLE BEGiNS TO MOVE UPWARDS, LiFTiNG THE SLEEPER TOWARDS THE iNEViTABLE moment of consciousness. The old man, however, was already awake. One of the penalties of growing old was the inability to sustain an unbroken night's sleep, he thought regretfully.

Now he lay in the darkness, listening to the noises of the night: the heating system gurgling to itself, the pattering of raindrops on the window, the soft, light snoring of the cat, curled up asleep at the foot of his bed.

Above Kirilovitch's head, the icons hung. The blue-robed Virgin and the solemn child in her arms. He knew they did not see what he saw, lying here in the darkness. Their eyes looked straight into the eyes of God. They saw glory and eternity and life everlasting. He saw nothing but darkness, thick and impenetrable.

He remembered the cardiologist in the Levallois hospital telling him that his blood pressure was too high, his heartbeat was irregular. That without surgery, he might not have much time left. As if he didn't already know. Soon, his eyes would open upon what the icons saw, he thought to himself. But not yet. Not just yet. *O God*, he prayed, *if you are there, if you are listening: hold back that eternal dawn for just a little longer. Let me live to finish this. Let me see their faces one more time in this world.*

NEXT MORNING JAZMIN WAS WOKEN UP BY THE SOUND OF RAIN LASHING DOWN OUTSIDE HER WINDOW. EVEN THE POXY WEATHER DIDN'T LIKE HER NOW, SHE THOUGHT DISGUSTEDLY. SHE CHECKED her watch: 6.45 a.m. Time to get vertical. She levered herself reluctantly upright and padded to the bathroom to begin her day.

"You're up very early this morning," Assia remarked as Jazmin slouched into the kitchen.

"Unh," Jazmin grunted. She hunted in the fridge, grateful that one of the properties of thickly applied mascara was its ability to glue one's eyes open.

"What's all this in aid of?"

"I'm going to school early to do some extra studying before class. Is that okay?"

Assia did a palms-up. "Hey, go for it."

Jazmin glugged down some juice. Actually, her real reason for arriving at school before everybody else was to avoid another public humiliation at the school gate.

Assia nodded encouragingly at her daughter. "So, have a nice day," she said. "Study hard. Do all your homework. I should be home early tonight. Will you be in for tea?"

Jazmin did a rapid forward-scan. She had told the old guy she'd stop by after school. She was going to introduce him to the concept of Christmas trees. "Yeah, I'll be back by five, maybe," she said vaguely.

Assia nodded. "I'll catch you later then. *Carpe diem*, eh!" she said, picking up her suit jacket from the back of the chair and going to pick up her briefcase. A second later, Jazmin heard the front door slam. Sheesh, sometimes her mum was truly weird, she thought, shaking her head sadly. Jazmin's life was spiralling into total meltdown, and her mum was wittering on about *carp*! Hel-*lo*, what planet was she from?

A few minutes later, Jazmin also hit the pavement. The rain had changed from "pour" to "spit". She hurried along, trying to ignore the queasy feeling in the pit of her stomach. She really ought to have thrown a sickie, she thought gloomily. As if to prepare herself for the unknown disasters of the day ahead, her mind started creating an imaginary scenario in which she, Jaz Dawson, super-heroine and kick-ass gorgeous crime fighter, was on a plane to Australia, when suddenly, the entire cabin crew and two pilots were struck down by a deadly virus.

Fortunately, she was able to leap forward, just as the plane was plummeting down towards total disaster, take over the controls and fly the panicking passengers safely and single-handedly all the way to Brisbane. As she successfully brought the plane to a smooth halt outside the terminal building, she could clearly hear the waiting crowds chanting her name: "*Jazmin, Jazmin.*"

"Jazmin, Jazmin! Wait up."

Jazmin returned to reality with a jolt. The crowd was not calling her name after all. Instead, it was someone who was walking behind her. She stopped and turned around to see who it was. Her face fell.

"Hey, how're you doing?" Zeb said. He smiled brightly.

Jazmin cut him a look that could have sliced logs. "Oh, it's *you*," she said coldly, pronouncing the word "you" in the same sort of way as she would the word "cockroach".

Zeb went on looking pleased to see her. "Are you going in early to study?" he inquired. "So am I."

"And this is any of your business because?" Jazmin snapped.

Zeb met her steely gaze straight on. He grinned back in a friendly way, totally oblivious to the messages she was sending him. Jazmin eye-rolled and clicked her teeth in exasperation. This was like trying to strike matches on jelly, she thought disgustedly. It was so obvious that Zeb Stone wouldn't recognize a big hint if it was dropped on him from a great height. She gave up and continued walking.

"Uh – so what did you do to your hand?" Zeb asked, falling into step next to her.

Jazmin looked down. She had cut her right thumb earlier on a knife as she attempted to hack some bread while half-asleep. The thumb was still bleeding. "It's nothing – a minor breakfast-related injury," she said shortly. She dug a grubby and shredded piece of tissue out of her pocket and buried her thumb in it.

Zeb tutted in a concerned way. "You're going to have trouble writing with that today," he commented.

"Yeah? Really? Am I? Bummer, eh."

They reached the gate. "So, see you around then," Jazmin said firmly. She waved a dismissive hand, striding off up the path in the direction of the entrance.

Zeb stopped. He stared after her, a puzzled expression on his face. Then: "Hey, wait," he called, running to catch her up once more.

Jazmin waited. She glared at him coldly, then looked pointedly from him to the gate and back again. "Well, excuse *me*," she said, doing a palms-up, "but shouldn't you be waiting for Honi to arrive?"

Zeb frowned. "I should? Why should I?"

Jazmin shook her head slowly from side to side. Honestly, she thought, for someone who lived life in the clever lane, Zeb was amazingly stupid. "Well, *duh* – because you're going out with her!" she told him witheringly.

Zeb looked confused. "No I'm not," he said. "Why do you say that?"

Jazmin scrutinized him narrowly. He looked genuine. Could he be telling her the truth? "You're not?" she inquired doubtfully.

"Uh-uh." Zeb shook his head.

"But she was boasting yesterday she had a date with you."

"Oh that. Yeah – she did ask me if I wanted to go see a movie with her, to say thanks for helping her with her maths. But then later I remembered we had a big family dinner scheduled, so I had to knock her back. Actually, just between you and me, I was quite glad of an excuse. I didn't want go out with her really. She's...um...unh...how can I put it –" Zeb stared up at the sky, as if seeking inspiration for the words he wanted.

An überwitch? The Intergalactic Queen of Darkness? Jazmin thought. She mentally wrestled the temptation to dive in and help him out.

"– not my type," Zeb finally came out with.

Jazmin felt her anger beginning to go melty at the edges, like a bar of chocolate that had been left out in the sun. Zeb had not been spidered into Honi's lair after all. Amazing. In her experience, most boys found Honi Delacy irresistible. It generally took them some time to join up the dots and realize there was a lot less to her than met the eye. Maybe she had got Zeb Stone wrong, she thought. She had been too judgy. Perhaps she should consider dropping the unfriendlies.

"And the other thing is, she never stops talking," Zeb went on. He paused: "She told me some weird stuff about you," he added.

Jazmin did a face-scrunch. "Yeah, I bet she did. You don't want to believe everything she says. That girl is a class-A liar."

"Hey, I didn't believe her," Zeb assured her earnestly. "Like, you'll never guess what? She told me you hadn't just joined the school this term, you'd actually been attending for years!"

Jazmin felt her cheeks going bright pink. "Oh. Uh, did she?" she stuttered.

"Whereas I clearly remember you telling me the very first time we met that you were new to the area."

"Err...I don't think I exactly said..."

"Hey, don't stress; I soon put her straight!" Zeb's face was a study in outraged indignation.

Jazmin hesitated momentarily, then she made a snap decision: "Look, why don't we go grab a drink or something," she said. "There's stuff I think I probably ought to tell you."

A SHORT TIME LATER, THREE PEOPLE COULD BE OBSERVED WALKING AROUND THE RETIREMENT COMMUNITY. ONE WAS THE SITE MANAGER, THE OTHER TWO ACCOMPANYING HIM WERE A MIDDLE-aged couple. The manager of the retirement community was talking volubly and with an enormous sense of pride.

"Notice that all walkways and footpaths are kept scrupulously clear of leaves," he said, indicating with a broad sweep of his arm. "Very important at this time of year. We know only too well the danger wet leaves underfoot can cause to our less agile residents."

The couple nodded understandingly. "Dad would appreciate that, wouldn't he?" the woman said, turning to her companion and linking her arm through his.

"He certainly would," the man agreed. "It all looks very nice."

The manager was impressed with these two. He saw many families in the course of his work, all eager to view the place where their elderly relatives might end their days, and he felt he could pick out the devoted from the merely dutiful. These two definitely came into the former category. They had made the appointment a couple of days ago, indicating that they were looking at a few retirement places in the area before selecting what they felt would suit their requirements.

They had informed him that the woman's father was in his sixties, still fit and active, but becoming less able to run the large family home on his own. The plan was to sell the house and invest some of the money in one of the retirement properties. So far, the couple had given every indication of being delighted with what they had been shown. They had praised the shopping facilities, the recreation and sports area, the medical centre and the entertainment complex. They had thoroughly approved of the CCTV camera at the entrance. "Security is so important nowadays, especially for the seniors," he'd told them, to more nods of approval.

Now, all that was left was to take a look at some of the properties designated in the glossy brochure as "senior singles". The site manager led the pleasantly spoken couple along a beech-chipping path, pointing out the clever use of evergreen shrubs to create all-year colour as they went. Eventually, they arrived at a cluster of single-storeyed dwellings.

"Here we are," he said, gesturing towards them. "Compact and cosy, but close to all amenities. Notice the use of solar panels, the ramped walkways and the recycling area."

As the couple stood noticing them, a small black and white cat suddenly shot out from under an evergreen shrub. It stalked, tail erect, up to one of the front doors, where it parked itself on the top of the ramp and set up a plaintive miaowing.

"You allow animals on the site?" the woman asked.

"Oh, well, yes. You know how our seniors love their pets," the manager replied.

The door slowly opened, to reveal an elderly-looking grey-haired man. He gave a quick, curious look at the visitors before letting the cat in. The woman's hand tightened upon the man's arm. The door closed. The woman leaned and whispered something into the man's ear.

The man turned to face the site manager. "Thank you

very much. I think we've seen everything we need to see now," he said briskly.

"Oh, really?" The manager was surprised. He hesitated. "Are you sure you don't want to look round one of the houses? Most people want to see what they're like inside."

"No, no, it all seems very nice," the man said decisively. He glanced sideways at his companion. "Doesn't it, dear?"

"Very nice indeed," the woman responded dutifully.

"So if you'll just direct us back to the car park," the man said, "we'll be on our way. As I said in my initial call, we have a few other places to visit today." He leaned forward and briefly touched the astonished site manager's sleeve. "I'm sure we'll be in touch again," he said and smiled. "One way or another."

The middle-aged couple found their car, drove out of the retirement complex and parked in a side street.

"That was lucky," the woman said.

"Damn lucky," the man grinned. He pulled a micro from his pocket. "I'll call and tell him the good news," he said. He punched in a set of numbers, waited. Then, "We found him, Mr. A!" he said.

The man started up the car engine, and the couple drove quickly away.

LATER THAT SAME AFTERNOON, JAZMIN WAS SITTING AT HER TABLE IN HER BEDROOM. SCHOOL WAS OUT, AND SHE HAD HER HEAD BENT DUTIFULLY OVER HER HOMEWORK. SHE HAD TAKEN ON BOARD what her mum had said. She was studying hard when her micro suddenly bleeped at her. Sighing, she picked it up off her desk and read the message: *RU wrkg?* Uttering a deep groan, she texted back: *Yes*. Then for good measure, she added: *Yes, YES, YES!!!* before switching the micro off, and throwing it irritably onto the bed behind her. This was the fourth time he'd contacted her, she thought crossly. It was tantamount to textual harassment.

It had seemed like such a brilliant idea, Jazmin thought wearily. Fess up to Zeb, clear the air, make a fresh start. And then in the course of her true confessions, she had unwittingly let slip how many assignments she had failed to complete, and how her mum had got discipliny. Zeb had immediately offered to help her with her maths, and she had accepted his kind offer. Duh! What she hadn't bargained for was how quickly he had also decided to take on the role of her life tutor too. Nor had she realized that he would enter into these roles with such focused and obsessive commitment, although from her observation of his rather odd and decidedly quirky personality, she should have guessed.

Jazmin rested her head in her hands. The irony was she had only agreed to accept Zeb's help because she felt guilty about not telling him the truth from the start, and also because she knew it would annoy Honi. Still, there was a positive side to all this, she thought. Something good was slowly emerging from the disaster.

For the first time in ages, Jazmin was experiencing a drastic distraction reduction. As a result, she was actually getting to grips with her studies. The pile of completed books on the floor was growing; the stratification on her desk was going steadily down. She had reached layers of homework that she had completely forgotten existed. In geological terms, she was now completing Precambrian assignments. Somewhere in the great cosmic system, she had to be racking up karmic brownie points, Jazmin told herself. She reached out her hand and picked up the next piece of work.

MEANWHILE, SEATED ON ONE OF THE PLUSH CRIMSON AND GOLD CHAIRS IN HIS MAYFAIR HOTEL ROOM, NIKOLAI ARKADY INITIATED A LONG-DISTANCE CALL TO HIS FATHER IN Ekaterinburg. Because they both knew that calls were being monitored, he had gone to some trouble to arrange for the call to be redirected through an untraceable number in New York. Nikolai made sure that he spent some time talking about his flight to JFK. He described the uptown hotel he was staying at (without actually naming it) and gave an outline of the business meeting he had attended that morning.

He also dropped the names of several fictitious colleagues into the conversation and finished up by describing to his father the swanky Manhattan bar he was now sitting in and the cocktail he had just ordered.

"Tomorrow, I shall visit Cartier, on Fifth Avenue," Nikolai told his father. "And then I will return to you shortly with a gift. You will, I think, be pleased with it. Yes. Very pleased indeed."

He rang off. Just an ordinary conversation. On the surface. Yet during the course of it, he had managed to convey to his father, in the pre-arranged code they had set up while he was still in Paris, the information that Ivan Kirilovitch had been located, and that plans were now well under way to eliminate him once and for all.

Nikolai Arkady smiled to himself. He could just imagine the frantic calls now being made from one ISA office to another, the wires running red hot, as the search to find him suddenly switched from Europe and moved continents. He picked up the phone a second time and rang room service. He ordered caviar, fillet steak with salad, and a bottle of Château-Neuf du Pape to be brought to his apartment. A working dinner. He still had many things to arrange before the "gift from Cartier" could be delivered.

THE LAST DAY OF THE CHRISTMAS TERM FOUND JAZMIN DAWSON STRUGGLING ALONG THE ROAD, CARRYING A HEAVY BAG. IT WAS FULL TO THE BRIM WITH COMPLETED ASSIGNMENTS. EVERY FEW steps, she was forced to stop, ease the bag off one aching shoulder and onto the other. In a better world, she'd get a big fat prize for all this, she thought to herself grimly. There was enough work in her bag to keep the facilitators busy for most of the Christmas holidays. Which served them jolly well right for setting it in the first place. Feeling in pain, but positive and girl-powery at the same time, Jazmin swept up the steps into the learning centre and began feeding the contents of her bag into the correct pigeonholes.

A few minutes later, her task completed, she picked up her now considerably lighter bag and paused, relishing for a couple of elusive seconds the unusual experience of a job well done. She had let things fester for far too long, she thought. It was great to feel fester-free. And today was definitely going to be a good day, she reminded herself. The learning centre closed early, so she was only going to have to be here until lunchtime. And her chief tormentors weren't even bothering to come in today. They'd taken the day off to go Christmas shopping. Oh joy. Humming happily and tunelessly to herself, Jazmin made her way to her first class.

MEANWHILE, AT THE RETIREMENT COMMUNITY, THE USUAL LINE OF VEHICLES WAS WAITING TO BE LET IN. HEADING UP THE QUEUE WAS A PINK JEEP BELONGING TO A COMPANY CALLED PRISCILLA'S Pretty Pampered Pooches. The fluffy blonde-haired girl at the wheel, who came every week to shampoo and trim the residents' dogs, spoke into the intercom. Then she sat and waited for the security guy in the admin block whose job it was to check the CCTV camera. When the barrier lifted, she revved her engine and drove the pink jeep into the complex.

The security guy checked in a local catering company and the laundry truck. Then the E-Z-Kleen Windows van arrived. It was let in too. Sometime later, a car containing the middle-aged couple drove past the retirement complex and parked in a nearby side street.

AT BREAKTIME, JAZMIN MET UP WITH ZEB IN THE CANTEEN.

"HEY, GUESS WHAT? I DID ALL MY ASSIGNMENTS," SHE TOLD HIM, GRINNING HAPPILY AS SHE SLIPPED INTO THE OPPOSITE SEAT. "And I handed them all in. Good, eh?" She unloaded her tray. It was treat time for Study-girl.

"Well done," Zeb said, nodding in a satisfied way. Jazmin could almost see him pulling out his mental clipboard and Olympic scorecards. Zeb unscrewed the top of a bottle of mineral water. Then he looked down at Jazmin's plate. Small frown lines started wandering across his brow. Uh-oh, Jazmin thought. Somewhere on a circuit board in Zeb's brain, a light had just started flashing.

"Please tell me you're not planning to eat that," Zeb said.

Jazmin sighed. She glanced at the glazed chocolate doughnut sitting innocently in front of her. Why did people have issues with her food choices? she thought wearily. "Yes, of course I'm going to eat it," she said. "Do you have a problem with that?"

Zeb shook his head and teeth-clicked disapprovingly. "Do you know how bad doughnuts are for you?"

Jazmin gave him a hard stare. "No," she said acidly. "And when did you join the Food Police?" she added.

Zeb ignored her. "Seriously, junk food is the reason why so many people on the planet are unhealthy," he told her earnestly.

Jazmin frowned. "What do you mean – junk food? Listen, Mr. I-Want-To-Heal-The-World, in case you didn't know, chocolate comes from a *plant*. So does sugar," she informed him, stabbing an index finger at the doughnut as she spoke. "Plants are *natural*. So what's your problem?"

"I'm just letting you know the facts, right."

"Yeah, yeah, what are you going to do about it?" Jazmin shrugged dismissively. She picked up the doughnut and took a deliberately large bite.

Zeb winced.

Jazmin chewed energetically. Zeb's top lip twitched.

"Look, quit hassling me," Jazmin told him in a rather muffled, chocolatey voice, "you're getting as bad as my mother."

Zeb patiently waited until she had demolished the doughnut. "So what are you planning to do after lunch?" he inquired.

Jazmin wiped chocolate from her mouth. "Nothing much," she shrugged. "I thought I might go see if my... umm...Great-Uncle Charles wants to do some Christmas shopping. Why?"

"I was going to suggest we did a bit more maths catch-up."

Jazmin waved her hands frantically in front of her. "Nonono! No more maths!" She shuddered.

"Okay, if you're quite sure." Zeb looked disappointed. He glanced at the canteen clock. "Well, time I visited the IRC," he said, picking up his bag and getting to his feet.

Her mouth falling open in shock and disbelief, Jazmin stared at him. "But it's the end of term!" she stuttered.

"Yes, I know – exactly the time when all the good textbooks get returned," Zeb said happily, his eyes gleaming. "I don't want to miss out on that, do I?"

THE E-Z-KLEEN WINDOW MAN LOOKED THROUGH THE GROUND-FLOOR WINDOW OF THE SMALL LIVING UNIT. HE SAW AN OLD MAN WITH IRON-GREY HAIR NAPPING IN AN EASY CHAIR, HIS LEGS covered by a brightly patterned red and green tartan rug. There was a black and white cat curled up peacefully on his lap. There was a red poinsettia on a small rosewood table. In one corner of the room, a small Christmas tree twinkled with coloured lights.

It was a really seasonal scene, the window cleaner thought to himself. Timeless in its picturesqueness. If you could have taken the lid off it, you'd have found some chocolates or possibly an interesting assortment of biscuits. It seemed a shame to disturb the old man's peace and quiet, but he had a job to do. He knocked gently on the window until the old man stirred, his eyes half-opening. The window cleaner held up his bucket, pointed to it, mimed turning on a tap.

Rubbing his eyes, the old man got unsteadily to his feet and went to open the kitchen door. The window cleaner was already standing on the threshold. He smiled in a friendly fashion. Then he reached down into the bucket and pulled out a gun.

THE MIDDLE-AGED COUPLE IN THE PARKED CAR SAT PATIENTLY IN SILENCE. THEY STARED OUT OF THE WINDSCREEN. AFTER A WHILE, THE MAN CHECKED HIS WATCH AND NODDED. "ANY MINUTE NOW," he muttered. A short time later, they heard the sound of police sirens wailing in the distance, getting closer every second.

"Right on cue," the man said. They waited a bit longer. Then the man got out of the car and walked round the corner. Five minutes passed, after which he reappeared and climbed back into the car.

"There appears to have been an 'incident'," the man told the woman. He grinned broadly. "There's a security guard at the entrance stopping cars from going in." He pulled out his micro, punched in a set of numbers and waited. "Looks like we got him, Mr. A," he said.

The man started up the car engine, and the couple drove swiftly away.

ASSIA WAS IN THE MIDDLE OF A TOP-LEVEL GOVERNMENT MEETING AT PORTCULLIS HOUSE WHEN THE MESSAGE CAME THROUGH FROM HALLY SKINNER, HER DEPUTY AT THE ISA HQ, THAT SHE NEEDED TO call her department urgently. Excusing herself, Assia went out into the foyer to make the call. "Hally?" she said when she got through. "What's going on?"

"Assia?" Hally sounded extremely agitated. "Thank goodness you called straight back. Listen, they've found a dead body at the retirement complex. It could be the Russian."

Assia's heart lurched.

"The body was found just outside the house where he's staying."

Assia felt the blood draining from her face. Her throat

went dry, and her legs started to shake uncontrollably. She felt the room beginning to spin around her. She leaned heavily on the desk to support herself. "Go on," she heard herself say in a voice she didn't recognize as hers.

"The police didn't give any further details," Hally said. "I just thought I'd better contact you as soon as I could. Will you go and do an ID?"

"Yes, of course. Call and tell them I'm on my way. Nobody should go near the body until I get there."

As if from a very long distance, Assia saw her hand calmly putting the phone down. Then, feeling like she had suddenly become part of some surreal nightmare, she walked slowly across the foyer and out into the street, where she hailed a cab. Giving the driver the address of the retirement community, she threw herself into the back and slammed the door.

As the cab bore her swiftly away, Assia slumped down in her seat. Technically she was not crying, she thought to herself. Nothing had left her eyes. But inside her, it felt as if a door had unlocked itself on a cold night. It had blown wide open, and the darkness and all the fearful things that inhabited it had come rushing in.

Assia's taxi was met at the community entrance by a senior police officer, who accompanied her on the short walk to the old man's house. Grey-faced and silent, Assia followed the officer up the beech path to the rear of the house, which was now a hive of police activity. Blue and white crime-scene tape festooned the approach. Temporary exclusion barriers were being erected. Neighbours were being questioned and comforted. A fingertip search of the immediate area had already started. A police pathologist was talking animatedly into her recorder as she waited for permission to begin her work, but as Assia drew near the house, her whole attention was focused upon the body, lying half in, half out of the open kitchen doorway. It was covered by a sheet.

"We've been informed that the man who lived at the house was a Mr. Charles Smith," the senior officer said, walking Assia towards the sheeted mound. "Is that right?"

Assia nodded.

"Can you tell us whether this is the same man?" the officer asked.

He bent down and pulled back the top half of the sheet. Reminding herself that identifying dead bodies was part of her job description and steeling herself for what she was about to view, Assia shut her eyes, took a few deep breaths, swallowed hard. Then she looked down: "But...this isn't him!" she gasped.

Assia Dawson stared at the unfamiliar features of the dead man, then raised her bewildered eyes to the senior officer's face. "I'm sorry, but I've never seen this man before in my life!" she said.

ARRIVING AT THE RETIREMENT COMMUNITY ENTRANCE SOME TIME
LATER, JAZMIN WAS PUZZLED TO DISCOVER THAT THERE WAS A
SECURITY GUARD AT THE BARRIER. TO HER CERTAIN KNOWLEDGE,
there had never been one before. She greeted him politely,
and was astonished when the security guard refused to let
her enter.

"But I've come to collect my great-uncle," she
protested. "We're going Christmas shopping together. He's
waiting for me."

The guard shook his head. "Nuh-uh," he told her.
"Nobody comes in until I get the order to let them in.
More than my job's worth to let you through."

Jazmin gave him a hard stare. She was just about to
open her mouth to protest, when a police car, siren
blaring, raced up to the barrier. The security guard
immediately raised the barrier and waved the driver
through. Jazmin followed the police car greedily with her
eyes as it swept up the short drive and disappeared round
a corner. Something was going on in there, she thought.
And it must be something majorly serious. Once more the
security guard looked down at her, his face full of his own
importance, and consequently, her insignificance.

"You still here, girlie?" he said. "I told you, you
can't come in right now. Why don't you go home and try
later?"

For a second, Jazmin hesitated. She seemed to be
thinking hard. Then, unexpectedly, she nodded up at him.

"Right. Yeah," she agreed, "why don't I go and do just that."

Jazmin walked away. Once out of sight of the security guard, however, she turned, retraced her steps, and began making her way quietly along the side of the high wooden fence that surrounded the community. There was always another way in, she thought. And when interesting stuff was happening, she owed it to herself to find out exactly what it was.

By the time Jazmin appeared on the scene, the pathologist had already begun examining the body. Assia was talking to some of the old man's neighbours, but as soon as she saw her daughter arrive she hurried over to her.

"Jazmin? What are you doing here?"

"I'm visiting," Jazmin said. "Like you told me to," she added pointedly. "Remember?"

"Oh yes. Of course." Assia was momentarily disorientated. She stared at her daughter distractedly, then was struck by her dishevelled appearance. "What on earth have you been up to?" She frowned, pulling small bits of broken wood from Jazmin's hair and dropping them on the ground.

"Um, it's nothing." Jazmin shook her head, adding more bits of wood and quite a few dead leaves to the collection at her feet. In the end, she'd discovered there was no other way into the complex, so she'd had to create one. She peered over her mum's shoulder. "Whoa – what's going on?"

"I'm afraid there's been a—"

"Hey, Mum. Is that a *body*?" Jazmin cut in, her eyes lighting up with interest. She craned her neck, trying to look over her mother's shoulder. Assia took her firmly by the elbow and walked her a short distance away.

"Omigod, it's not...?" Jazmin began.

Her mum shook her head. "No, it isn't," she said. "Now listen, hon, it's not a good idea for you to be here. Someone, we think he might have been a window cleaner, has been shot. The police don't know how it happened yet. It's remotely possible that the gunman could still be lurking somewhere, so I'd like you to go straight home right now."

"Where's—"

"We don't know. Possibly he's just gone for a walk or a visit."

"Okay. You don't think anything bad's happened to him?"

"Right now, I'm trying to keep an open mind about everything," Assia said firmly.

"But he hasn't turned up."

Assia shook her head. "Not yet."

"Whoa – maybe he's been kidnapped or something?"

"Go," Assia said. She put her hands on Jazmin's shoulders and gave her a gentle push in the right direction.

"Yeah, yeah, I'm going," Jazmin said. She turned and walked along the beech path that led to the front gate. Her Spidey-sense was telling her there was more to this than her mum was letting on. Jazmin waited until she was out of sight. Then she stopped walking. Go straight home? As if. Jaz Dawson, her imaginary, kick-ass, gorgeous alter-ego would never wimp out on a mission. It was time to do some sleuthing. Engaging lurkage mode, she began to creep back along the path.

HAVING SEEN HER DAUGHTER SAFELY ON HER WAY, ASSIA RETURNED TO WHAT WAS NOW CLEARLY A MURDER INVESTIGATION. SHE JOINED A SILENT GROUP OF POLICE OFFICERS WHO WERE gathered round the white-suited pathologist. Everyone was watching her carrying out her grisly tasks on the dead body. Suddenly, the pathologist looked up. "Aha. Interesting. Very interesting," she murmured.

Assia and one of the senior police officers exchanged meaningful glances. What was it about pathologists? Assia wondered. It must be something to do with the nature of their work that meant they so enjoyed their moment in the spotlight. And they were always such infuriating drama queens. You had to coax information out of them slowly, piece by precious piece.

"What is it?" she asked.

The pathologist straightened up and sat back on her

heels. She was holding something small in her blue-gloved hand. "Here," she said. "Take a look at this."

Assia glanced down. "Right. It's a cartridge."

"It's a *nine-millimetre* cartridge," the pathologist corrected, her eyes gleaming. She rolled the small piece of metal round in her palm, looking up at Assia and waiting.

Assia sighed and eye-rolled. "And its significance is?" she asked.

The pathologist smiled smugly. "The gun found near the body is a .22 Smith & Wesson automatic."

"Ah."

The pathologist inclined her head. "Ah indeed. The bullet that killed your man has come from another weapon," she said. And closed her mouth firmly.

"Anything else?" Assia asked, mentally knuckle-crunching.

The pathologist pursed her lips. "It's an unusual sort of bullet," she offered.

"You're saying?"

"I'd guess the gun that fired it was probably foreign."

Assia felt her heart lurch uncomfortably. "Could it be Russian?" she suggested, voicing her worst fear.

The pathologist shrugged. "Possibly. A Makarov might fire nine-millimetre cartridges. Of course, I couldn't definitely commit to that," she said tartly. "You'd have to consult one of my colleagues in ballistics."

Assia nodded, then turned away. She walked off a few

paces, trying to make some sense of what was happening. One of the police officers approached her.

"We found this on the ground near the house," he said, holding out a clear plastic bag containing a silver watch. The glass was smashed. "Do you know anything about it?"

Assia stared at the watch, recognizing it instantly as the one she'd given Kirilovitch. All at once, she felt sick. So it looked like the old man had not wandered off, he had been snatched. Jazmin's wild assumptions were not so far-fetched after all. Instantly, Assia's mind began working out a possible scenario: someone must have taken Kirilovitch at gunpoint, she told herself, ruthlessly shooting down and killing an innocent window cleaner, who presumably had tried his best to protect him. The Russian gun meant that the kidnapper had to be linked to one man: Nikolai Arkady. He must have recognized the old man on that Paris street and, somehow, he'd managed to track him down, and had arranged for him to be lifted right under their noses. The New York phone call had just been a clever ruse, something to lull them into a sense of false security, she thought angrily.

Assia bunched her left hand into a fist and smashed it into her right palm. This had happened on her watch, so it was her responsibility. There were no words for how she was feeling right now. She had promised the old guy that he would be safe, and she had broken her promise. She shook her head in blank disbelief. She had done everything right, but somehow, despite her best efforts, she had lost him. And with him had gone access to the vital piece of evidence. And now a vulnerable old man was out there somewhere, his life in grave danger, and she had no idea how she could find him.

AFTER EVERYONE HAD GONE, JAZMIN EMERGED FROM HER HIDING PLACE BEHIND THE RECYCLING BINS. SHE HAD SAT AND WATCHED THE BODY BEING BAGGED AND TAKEN AWAY, THE SITE BEING TAPED and the police loading themselves into their cars and leaving. Now it was quiet and peaceful and time for her to start her investigations.

Jazmin approached the police officer by the barrier, assuming an innocently helpful expression. "Hi," she smiled, looking up at him wide-eyed.

The police officer, who was young and eager to be efficient, slowly folded his arms, and drew himself up to his full height.

"Yes? Can I help you?" he inquired in a crisp, I'm-very-important voice.

Jazmin's smile widened. "I need to feed the cat," she told him.

The officer hesitated. Nobody had mentioned a cat or its feeding arrangements. He scrutinized Jazmin from head to toe. She seemed harmless enough. But he had his orders.

"Nobody's allowed inside," he said.

Jazmin's smile never wavered. "So who's going to feed it, then?"

The officer frowned. He held a quick mental debate with himself. Small girl. Cat. Food. He checked the time. He wasn't due to be relieved for another hour.

"Well..." he began.

"Thanks. I won't be long." Jazmin quickly ducked under the barrier and pushed open the door. It had swung shut behind her before the young officer could finish his sentence.

Once inside, she performed a swift walk-through, doing an initial recce. The kitchen had been dusted for fingerprints, but apart from that, everything seemed fine. Nothing out of the ordinary. Nothing to suggest that a vicious crime had occurred on the premises only a short time previously. Naturally, there was no sign of Tolstoy, but she remembered the old man telling her that the cat liked to hang out under bedroom furniture when it was scared.

Jazmin went to the bedroom, kneeled down and peered under the bed. Sure enough, two eyes met hers in an unblinking green stare. "Hey, there you are," she said. She stretched out her hand and tried to lure the cat out with few encouraging chirrups. It treated her to a withering look and made no attempt to move.

Jazmin sat down beside the bed. "You know what," she remarked, "if all this happened in a kid's novel, I'd be asking you what went on and you'd actually talk to me and tell me." She paused for a few seconds, eyeing the cat speculatively. Just in case. It eyed her back, impassive and silent. Eventually, Jazmin did a palms-up. "Yeah, you're probably right," she said, getting to her feet. "I never believed in those stupid kids' books anyway. Much better if I take a good look around and work it out for myself, yeah?"

Jazmin subjected the old guy's house to a longer and more careful scrutiny, noting down anything she regarded as important. Then she filled the cat's dish with food and refreshed the water bowl and let herself out of the front door.

STRAIGHT AFTER COMPLETING HER INITIAL INVESTIGATIONS, JAZMIN HEADED FOR THE NEAREST COFFEE SHOP. THIS WAS DEFINITELY GOING TO BE A TWO-COOKIE PROBLEM, SHE THOUGHT TO herself. She chose a pecan 'n' walnut and an M&M, paid at the till and carried the plate over to a vacant table. In the crime novels she read, the great detectives always employed logic, deduction or intuition to solve their problems. Mostly, she solved her problems with food.

Breaking the first cookie into bite-sized chunks, Jazmin tried to make some sense out of what had happened. A missing old man. A dead body. It certainly was a mystery. Think, girl, think, she told herself. Look at what you saw.

Jazmin threw up a mental picture of the interior of the house and started walking herself round it for a third time. Somewhere, there had to be a clue as to what had happened.

She tried to put herself in the old man's shoes, to visualize the actual moment of capture. If somebody tried to kidnap her, what would she do? Nothing. She wouldn't have time. Suddenly, Jazmin sat bolt upright. She popped the last piece of cookie into her mouth and crunched it loudly. Of course! The answer had been staring her in the face all the time. Or rather, it hadn't!

A COUPLE OF MINUTES LATER, THE PHONE ON ASSIA'S DESK SHRILLED LOUDLY, BREAKING THE UNSPOKEN TENSION THAT HAD BEEN GATHERING IN THE OFFICE, LIKE DARK STORM CLOUDS, ALL afternoon. Cutting her eyes at her deputy, Hally, Assia grabbed the phone and punched the recording monitor. Then she propped her chin in her hand and listened carefully to the voice at the other end. Hally stopped typing and stared fixedly across the desk. She watched as Assia tried vainly to slide the odd word into the one-sided conversation happening at the other end of the phone.

Finally and abruptly, the caller rang off.

"Was it the kidnappers? What did they say?" Hally asked eagerly.

For a moment, Assia sat without moving, a look of

bemusement on her face. Then she bent her head, ran both hands through her hair and groaned loudly.

Hally looked concerned. "That bad, huh?"

Assia raised her head. "It wasn't the kidnappers," she sighed. "It was Jazmin."

"Oh." Hally pulled a face. She was a bit twitchy about Assia's daughter. The memory of the clever trick Jazmin had pulled on her last summer when she'd managed to get herself to Prague lingered on and festered. "Lost her lunch money, has she?" she remarked sarkily.

Assia sighed exasperatedly. "She's been poking around Kirilovitch's house. I told her to go home, but as usual she developed selective deafness and ignored me. She says she had to go back and check on the cat."

Hally clicked her teeth.

"Honestly, I think that girl was born without brakes," Assia grumbled.

Hally cut her a sympathetic glance.

"Now she says that Kirilovitch has definitely not been kidnapped."

Hally's mouth formed a thin line of disapproval. "Uh-huh. Why does she say that?"

"She's noticed that all his icons have gone, and his library book isn't there."

"Excuse me?"

"She says you wouldn't have time to pack anything if you were being kidnapped."

A deep frown line appeared between Hally's brows.

Assia picked up a pen and twirled it round between her fingers like a baton. "Oh dear. I don't know what to think," she said.

Hally's expression spoke volumes.

"I know," Assia said, shrugging. "But she seems very convinced."

"*Library book?*" Hally smiled, waving a dismissive hand. "*Icons?*" She leaned across the desk. "Teenagers, huh! They watch far too much TV, then think they know all about everything!" She rose to her feet. "I'll go get you a cup of tea. Seems like you're having a *really* stressful day!"

Hally got up and left the office. Assia reached wearily for her "To do" list and rechecked it. She had alerted all airports and ports in case whoever was holding Kirilovitch tried to take him out of the country. She had checked with the NYPD and urged them to prioritize tracing the call Nikolai made to his father. She had contacted the Metropolitan Police and Scotland Yard, and put i-pics of Nikolai and of Kirilovitch on the Interpol website. She had done everything she possibly could to find him, even though a small insistent voice in her head kept telling her that she was wasting her time. The old man was already dead, his body dumped on some waste ground or piece of scrubland. But Assia refused to listen. She wasn't going to go there. Not yet.

THAT NIGHT, JAZMIN LAY IN THE DARK, HER ARMS FOLDED BEHIND HER HEAD. SHE STARED UP AT THE CEILING. WHAT WAS IT WITH ADULTS? SHE WONDERED. YOU TOLD THEM SOME MADE-UP STORY that was so far over the reality line that they needed a telescope, and they believed every darn word. You told them the truth, and they raised their eyebrows, smiled indulgently and didn't believe you. She pulled a face in the darkness. She hated it when her mum went all unlisteny on her. Especially just now, when she was clearly beating herself up over what she thought had happened to the old man.

Jazmin was pretty sure she had solved the mystery of Kirilovitch's disappearance. Sure, there were some unanswered biggies like "Who Shot the Window Cleaner?" and "Why?" But as every good secret agent knew, that was the way mysteries tended to go. There was no such thing as a small mystery. Not for long. Mysteries got bigger. They were like amoebae: they multiplied.

And there was another thing that backed up her theory, she thought. Since making her breakthrough discovery earlier, she had remembered something else: the conversation she'd had with Kirilovitch way back at the chess game. She recalled how he'd told her that being surrounded by books made him feel safe. How he used to spend a lot of time in libraries.

Jazmin unfolded her arms and rolled over onto her side. Tomorrow was the first day of the Christmas holidays, and she was going to spend it staking out the library. The irony did not escape her. Sighing, she pulled the duvet up to her chin. It was going to be a very cold night. She hoped the old man had found somewhere warm and safe to stay.

MEANWHILE, ON THE OTHER SIDE OF LONDON, THE SOUP-RUN VAN WAS MAKING ITS LAST VISIT OF THE NIGHT: ELEVEN THIRTY, THE ARCHES UNDER CHARING CROSS STATION. THE YOUNG VOLUNTEERS let down the side hatch and got ready for business. They stirred the steaming metal vats of hot soup, checked the sandwiches and lined up the plastic cups for tea and coffee. Meanwhile, the remnants of humanity who inhabited the cardboard boxes (if they were lucky) or slept on the bare pavement, assembled themselves in a ragged line and waited for their supper.

There was very little conversation in the queue and practically no eye contact. As each bedraggled figure appeared at the hatch, the volunteers announced the menu – tonight it was chicken and vegetable soup, a choice of cheese or ham sandwiches, tea and coffee. A muttered request was uttered, and the food handed down to hands that shook uncontrollably and were blue with cold or stained black with nicotine and filth.

The line of customers had come and gone, and the volunteers were beginning to pack away, when someone else appeared at the serving hatch. He carried a bag – an almost unheard-of item among the tattered humanity that had just muttered and mumbled around the van. A tartan blanket was slung jauntily, bandolier style, across his shoulders. He was warmly dressed, and, most unusual of all, he made eye contact and he didn't smell.

"I gather I can get some food here?" the old man said. His voice was clipped, precise.

The volunteers, trained not to question, served the old man with a cup of hot soup, a round of cheese sandwiches. He politely declined a cup of tea. Then, having eaten and enjoyed his food, he thanked them and set off in the direction of the Strand. The volunteers watched him go.

After he had disappeared from view, they packed up the van. Another successful soup run completed. Tomorrow, they would be out again. And the old man? Maybe he would come. Maybe not. It was hard surviving on the streets in the depth of December. The volunteers silently wished him luck. He would need it.

SOMETIME LATER, THE OLD MAN WAS SITTING IN THE DARKENED DOORWAY OF A BIG STORE, SURROUNDED BY HIS FEW POSSESSIONS. HE HAD BEEN RICH, HE THOUGHT TO HIMSELF, AND HE HAD BEEN poor. Rich was definitely better, but right now poor was not without its plus points: nobody could track him down. No strangers with guns, no organization that had promised to protect him but had singularly failed to do so.

He had become anonymous, invisible. Nobody would give him a second glance. He was a blanketed shape in a doorway, just another piece of street detritus. Now there was only the sky above him and what he carried in his two hands.

He looked up at the sky, glowing soft orange in the lights of the city. The stars were out, he could just see them, tiny pinpricks of silver. There was a timeless quality to them. The same stars had been in place for thousands of years, he reflected. They had shone down on him during that cold, mind-numbing trudge through the snow to Perm. They would shine still when he was dead and gone. In the light of their permanence, he felt suddenly insignificant. As if his life meant nothing. As if he was merely a microscopic grain of dust on the mirror of eternity.

He shivered, pulling the blanket closer around his shoulders to shut out the cold. He leaned against the plate-glass window, curling his body into itself, trying to position himself so as to make the most of the warm air coming up from the basement vent. High above his head, the sparkly Christmas lights on the front of the big department store flashed on and off, on and off, while bright luminous plastic angels lifted their glittery trumpets, sending up a silent fanfare to the night sky. Man's response to the magnificence of heaven. *Season's Greetings,* they proclaimed. *Goodwill to All. Happy Holiday to Our Customers.*

IT WAS EARLY THE NEXT MORNING. SO EARLY INDEED, THAT IT WAS ALMOST LATE THE NIGHT BEFORE. THE OLD MAN WAS AWAKE AND FEELING STRANGELY, ILLOGICALLY HAPPY. HE SAT UPRIGHT, leaning his back against the side of the building and hugging his knees with his arms. Unusually, given the circumstances, he had slept well, sailing into a sea of sleep so black and wide that it had no features and no shape and was enlivened by no dreams.

He had been woken up by the noise of an early morning delivery truck grinding its way slowly down the street. The sky was a deep and glorious royal blue, fading to turquoise and forget-me-not in the east, where dawn was nudging the city skyline. The air smelled crisp and fresh and encouraging.

Now he breathed in deeply. Once again, he had survived an attack upon his life, he thought. He was still here, and best of all, he was free to explore all the possibilities that the day and the city offered. For a moment longer he sat motionless, savouring the unaccustomed sense of triumph. Then he rolled up the tartan rug. Stuffing it into his bag, he stood up and sniffed the cold, refreshing air like an old warhorse scenting battle. Feeling almost euphoric, he picked up his few possessions and ambled off in search of some breakfast.

AT SEVEN FIFTEEN, JAZMIN WOKE UP, HIT THE SHOWER AND BEGAN HER CAREFUL PREPARATIONS FOR THE STAKE-OUT. SHE PUT ON HER BLACK COMBATS, A THICK BLACK POLO TOP, HER GREEN QUILTED body warmer and her black boots. Ever since she'd hung out with ISA agents Stash McGregor and Suki Smith last summer in Prague, she'd wanted to dress like they did. Except that their body warmers were made of bulletproof Kevlar and they both worked out, so the effect on them was muscle-ripply and intimidating. Jazmin looked about as scary as a whelk.

She zipped her boots, checked herself in her bedroom mirror and did a nose wrinkle. Pity it was mid-December, she thought, because this outfit seriously needed a pair of dark designer wraparounds to give it that final authentic touch. She decided to take her wraparounds anyway. Just in case.

Now all she had to decide was what to do with the major hassle that was her hair. Jazmin ran her fingers through the curly, tangled mess. She should really have washed it last night, she thought regretfully. Too late now. She tried a few styles, then decided to tie the unruly mop back in a half-assed ponytail which she could stuff into a beanie. Best she could do. She gave herself a final once over: "Hey, five-by-five," she told herself. One spy girl, set and ready to go. She smiled at her reflection in the mirror, and gave herself a quick triumphant thumbs-up.

Jazmin migrated to the kitchen, where she got herself

some breakfast. Then she set about the final and most important of her preparations: provisions for the day. She made herself a stack of peanut butter and honey sandwiches, snagged some fruit, a packet of chocolate wholemeal biscuits and a big bottle of still water from the cupboard and packed everything away into her bag. On a stake-out, it was essential to have one's food supply to hand. She did not want things getting developmenty while she was queuing at a lunch counter.

JAZMIN TOTED HER BULGING BAG OUT INTO THE EARLY-MORNING STREET. OF COURSE, IN AN IDEAL WORLD, SHE MIGHT ALSO HAVE PACKED SUCH ESSENTIALS AS DEFENCE SPRAY, STUN GUN, CUFFS and a cool weapon, she thought sorrowfully. However, she consoled herself with the thought that all this extra equipment would only take up the valuable space needed for the other detecting essentials, like handheld, torch, string, roll of mints and sticks of gum. She hustled along the pavement. It was important to get to the library before it opened, as she needed to secure one of the coveted single desks within sight of the entrance.

Reaching the library, Jazmin ran a quick ID check on the people queuing outside the building. Even though it was only five past nine, there was already a small crowd waiting to go in, consisting of desperate, baggy-eyed mothers with wriggly small children and the usual group of early-rise seniors who seemed to live permanently in the reading room. She knew they would make a beeline for the easy chairs and the daily papers as soon as the doors opened.

Jazmin stood and waited. Kirilovitch's book, the one he'd borrowed on the day of the chess competition, was due back today. That was why she was sure he'd call in. No serious library user ever returned their books late if they could avoid it; the fines were extortionate. And he'd taken the book out on someone else's ticket too. Her ticket. He had a moral obligation to return it on time. And he didn't actually have anywhere else to go, did he?

At nine thirty precisely, the big double doors slid back and the crowd surged forward. Jazmin headed straight for the study areas. The carrel nearest the door was free. Hey, good seating karma, she thought; it had to be a sign. She dumped her bag onto the chair to reserve her place and went to return her books at the counter.

THREE HOURS LATER, JAZMIN WAS STILL SITTING AT HER DESK, WAITING FOR SOMETHING TO HAPPEN. NOTHING WAS. FUNNY HOW STAKE-OUTS ALWAYS SEEMED SO MUCH MORE EXCITING IN BOOKS and films, she mused wryly. The time seemed to zoom by. The stakee always turned up well before the staker's patience ran out. Meanwhile, back in the real world, she was bored, hungry and needed the bathroom.

Jazmin considered her options: but if she left for a break

now, she ran the risk that the old guy would show up while she was gone. On the other hand, if she stayed here much longer, she might pass out with starvation. She couldn't eat her lunch in the library – eating and drinking was strictly forbidden. What she needed was a trusty sidekick, she thought to herself. Someone who was pretty gullible and would be quite happy to hang out in the library for a while. Someone who wasn't likely to be tempted away by a sudden snack-attack or an overwhelming desire to shop. And – oooh, guess what? – she reckoned she knew the very person to ask. Jazmin flipped open the lid of her micro and began texting.

WHILE JAZMIN WAS WAITING PATIENTLY FOR HER TRUSTY SIDEKICK TO TURN UP, ASSIA WAS WAITING WITH GROWING IMPATIENCE FOR THE PHONE CALL THAT WOULD LET HER KNOW WHAT HAD happened to the old man. The NYPD had traced Nikolai's call to a bar in Manhattan and were now sweeping the big hotels in case he'd registered under a false name. Not that his location would prove anything, she thought. Long experience had taught her that a man with money and the right contacts could arrange almost anything anywhere.

While she waited, Assia was writing up an incident report for her boss. She had just completed one for the police. There was also a complicated form to fill in for the manager of the retirement community. Assia sighed. The old man had gone. Stash and Suki had not yet located his wife and daughter. Nikolai Arkady seemed to have vanished off the face of the earth. Nothing was happening except paperwork. She should be out on the street, hustling for information. Instead she was stuck in the office waiting for the phone to ring and drinking endless latte grandes, which were only making her even more hyped up and twitchy.

"SO," ZEB SAID IN HIS INFURIATINGLY METHODICAL WAY, "LET ME GET THIS ABSOLUTELY STRAIGHT: YOUR GREAT-UNCLE CHARLES HAS BEEN MISSING SINCE YESTERDAY. YOU DON'T KNOW WHERE HE'S gone, and you're waiting to see if he turns up here?"

"Got it in one."

"Have you tried calling him?"

Jazmin hit her forehead with her open palm. "Well duh! How come *I* didn't think of that?"

Zeb looked pleased. Then he caught the sarcastic expression on her face and his smile faded. "Only trying to help," he said.

Jazmin eye-rolled. "Sure you were."

"So I guess his micro's switched off?"

"You got it. Like I told you, I think something bad happened where he's staying." Jazmin had decided not to mention the dead man quite yet. "I think he got scared and that's why he took off. And then maybe he got lost or something, I'm not sure. Mum says he's a bit vague sometimes, on account of being old. But he likes libraries," she went on. "And I let him borrow a book on my ticket, and it's due today." It sounded like a fairly convincing story, she thought, so long as you didn't factor in things like logic or common sense.

"Oh well, if his book is due today, then he'll definitely show up," Zeb, the consummate bibliophile said, nodding earnestly.

"So you're okay to hang around for a bit while I grab some fresh air and a break?"

"Sure. No problem. Hey, this is just like one of those stake-out things you see in films, isn't it?"

"Mmmh," Jazmin said cautiously. She really didn't want to get his imagination started.

"Whoa, it's all rather exciting," Zeb went on. He grinned at her. "I never thought I would be taking part in a real live stake-out today. Do you think I should borrow your wraparounds in case anybody recognizes me?"

Jazmin groaned. Once again, Zeb was taking his responsibilities absolutely literally and far too seriously. There was only room for one imaginary kick-ass secret agent around here. She gave him a stern look.

"What do I do if I see him?" Zeb continued, his eyes gleaming behind his glasses. "Should I shout 'Freeze!' and go into that squatting cop stance?"

Jazmin gritted her teeth. "Ha ha, very amusing. Why

don't you just sit here until I come back, okay?" she told him, pushing him firmly down into his seat. "Call me if you see my great-uncle."

JAZMIN HURRIED OUT OF THE LIBRARY AND HEADED FOR THE GROUND FLOOR OF THE SHOPPING MALL. AFTER MAKING A MUCH NEEDED VISIT TO THE BATHROOM, SHE FOUND HERSELF A BENCH TO perch on and started to devour her lunch. The mall was crowded with Christmas shoppers. Kids were screaming and throwing themselves round the indoor ice rink. The stores were bright with coloured lights and tinsel, and the air rang with jolly piped Christmas music.

Jazmin watched the crowds passing in and out of the stores, consulting lists, selecting gifts. Only a short time until Christmas, she thought, and she still hadn't bought a single present. Nor written a single card. She hadn't even got any idea what to get her mum. It was tragicistan: if she didn't get her act together, Christmas was going to turn up and find her totally unprepared.

Stuffing down her final sandwich, Jazmin got up and wandered into one of the big stores in search of inspiration. She wanted to buy her mum something really special this year, for a change, she thought to herself. Too often in the past, they hadn't been getting on. However, she was beginning to see their relationship differently now, and for once, she wanted to put some thought into her mum's present. She decided to allow herself a quick look round before returning to the library. Just to get some ideas.

Coming out of the store, some time later, Jazmin realized how much time had passed since she'd left Zeb on his own. Feeling slightly guilty, she power-walked herself straight back to the library. She barrelled through the door, a breezy apology already rising to her lips. But the words died in her throat; the apology remained unuttered.

The desk by the door was empty. Zeb Stone had gone.

FOR A BRIEF MOMENT, JAZMIN WAS STUNNED. THEN HER ANGER FLARED. SO MUCH FOR HER RELIABLE SIDEKICK! THANKS A LOT, PAL! UNH! HOW COULD HE HAVE LET HER DOWN? SHE'D ONLY BEEN gone for an hour and a half max, and it wasn't as if she'd asked him to do anything really complicated – all he had to do was sit and wait! Jazmin fumed. She hauled her micro out from her bag. That loser Zeb Stone was going to know *exactly* how she felt about him! She flipped the lid. The message light was on. She read the message. It said: *In cafe + g.uncle. Zeb.*

JAZMIN HURRIED INTO THE CAFÉ AND PICKED HER WAY BETWEEN THE CROWDED TABLES. KIRILOVITCH WAS SITTING BY THE WINDOW, CALMLY EATING A BOWL OF SOUP. ZEB WAS SITTING OPPOSITE, watching him.

"Er...hi," Jazmin said brightly, dropping into a chair. "Got your message."

The old man shot Zeb a reproachful look. "I thought we had an agreement," he said.

Jazmin looked at him, then she looked at Zeb. "Sorry?" she said. "Am I missing something here?"

Kirilovitch set down his spoon and sighed.

"He didn't want me to contact you," Zeb said apologetically. He looked faintly embarrassed.

"Why not?" Jazmin asked sharply. She stared at the old man, suddenly noticing the dishevelled state of his clothes, his unshaven face, the grime under his fingernails. "Hey, what happened to you?" she asked, her voice softening.

"He's been sleeping rough," Zeb told her.

Jazmin blinked. "Oh wow – poor you," she breathed.

Kirilovitch shrugged. Then he picked up his spoon and calmly went on with his soup.

Zeb and Jazmin watched him eat in silence.

When the bowl was empty, Jazmin looked at him expectantly. "So...?"

Kirilovitch sighed deeply. He cleared his throat. "I was having a little nap after my mid-morning tea," he said. "Someone tapped on the window. It was a window cleaner," he paused. His brow furrowed. "At least I thought that's who he was. He had a bucket, you see. Window cleaners usually carry buckets, don't they?"

"Yeah, yeah, they do," Jazmin agreed hastily. "Go on."

The old man stared thoughtfully into the middle distance. "It was a red bucket, as I recall."

"Fine. It was a red bucket. And then...?"

"And then I opened the back door..." His voice trailed off into silence.

Jazmin eye-rolled and cut him an exasperated look. Why was this taking so long? "Right. Okay. So you opened the back door, the window cleaner was there, with his bucket – his RED bucket," she added pointedly. "And then..."

The old man was staring straight ahead now, deliberately not making any eye contact with either of them. "He had a gun," he said, his voice flat and expressionless. "It was hidden in the bucket. He was going to shoot me. But I had my old Makarov – I always carry it on me, ever since I left Russia. And so I...I..."

"*Omigod, you shot him?*" Jazmin gasped.

Kirilovitch's gaze transferred itself to the table. His hands were shaking uncontrollably. "I had no choice: he pulled his gun on me first. When I was in the army, we were taught two simple rules: never pull out a gun unless you intend to shoot; never shoot unless you mean to kill."

"*I don't believe it – you SHOT him!*"

Zeb noticed the hands. He cut Jazmin a quick warning look. "Umm...maybe we shouldn't dwell on this right now, huh. It was obviously self-defence, right?"

Kirilovitch stared at him. "Do you think that's how the authorities will see it?" he said dubiously. "There were no

witnesses, you see. Nobody to confirm what happened."
He gave Jazmin a wary glance. "That's why I didn't want
Zeb to call you. I didn't want..." he paused, swallowed,
"anybody to worry. I don't want to end up getting arrested
by the police."

"Hey, I'm absolutely sure that won't happen," Zeb
assured him solemnly. "Will it?" he added, sending Jazmin
an "Agree with me" look.

But Jazmin was in another place altogether. "Whoa –
you mean you actually carry a gun?"

Kirilovitch nodded sadly.

"Umm...so, how have you been?" Zeb asked, shooting
Jazmin another meaningful glance.

"All right, I guess." The old man shrugged.

"Does my mum know you've got a gun?"

"It must have been very cold sleeping rough," Zeb
remarked, pointedly blanking Jazmin.

"I survived," the old man told him drily.

"I bet right now you could do with a hot shower," Zeb
remarked, kicking Jazmin under the table.

"You know, that would be wonderful."

Zeb turned and looked at Jazmin, who was still staring
at Kirilovitch.

"Look, please can we forget about what's happened for
now," Zeb said patiently. "How about we concentrate on
the present instead: your great-uncle needs a hot shower."

Reluctantly Jazmin dragged herself away from her gun-toting fantasy. "Yes, of course he does. I'm sorry. Look, why don't you come back to my place?" she suggested.

The old man looked worried again. "Your mother...?"

"My mother's at work," Jazmin said, adding quickly, "and I think she's got a late meeting tonight, so she won't be back until at least eight thirty, so you're quite safe."

Kirilovitch's expression was wooden. "I don't want her to know where I am. I don't want anyone to know," he stated firmly.

"But you can't..." Jazmin began, then stopped herself abruptly. "Okay, right, whatever. So let's go, shall we?"

Jazmin and Zeb walked the old man back to Jazmin's building, keeping one each side of him. Zeb carried his things and kept up an easy flow of conversation, for which Jazmin was thankful. She remained silent. Now that the old man had turned up, she had important issues of an ethical nature to think through. Loyalty issues, like whether she should contact her mum. And what she should say. Jazmin knew the old man had acted in self-defence. But a gun? She wasn't sure how her mother would react to that startling piece of news. It would need to be carefully handled.

As they walked, Jazmin cut Kirilovitch covert glances. She had clearly misjudged him. He might look and act like an old wrinkly, but he'd managed to defend himself against an armed intruder. And then survive a night on the street. The old man was a legend; he deserved total respect.

As soon as they reached the apartment, she directed him upstairs to the mezzanine. "You go have a shower, and I'll see about some more food. There are guest towels in the cupboard on the landing. Help yourself."

Unexpectedly, the old man reached out and let his hand rest lightly on her shoulder. "Thank you, Jazmin," he said quietly, looking at her. "I am very grateful." Then he turned and stomped off to the bathroom.

For a moment, Jazmin and Zeb stood in the hallway, watching him awkwardly mount the wooden stairs. As soon as he reached the bathroom door, Jazmin went to check out the meal situation. Zeb followed her into the sparkling clean kitchen, his eyes immediately lighting up with the bright, focused, interested expression that she had come to recognize and dread.

"So you can cook?" he asked. "That's great. I really like cooking as well."

Jazmin felt her heart sink. Why was Zeb so annoyingly enthusiastic about everything?

"Do you have any specialities?" Zeb continued happily. "I do an excellent strawberry shortcake. And I can also make lasagne with tossed green salad."

Her face expressionless, Jazmin opened the freezer. "Actually, I have three specialities," she said, "I thaw, I microwave and I order in." She reached for a packet of frozen pizzas. "Sort these for me, will you?" she commanded briskly, and she thrust the ice-encrusted package into his hands.

Jazmin left Zeb to do kitcheny things while she returned to the hallway. Upstairs in the bathroom, she could hear the clean white noise of the power-shower, as the old man unsuspectingly washed away the grime of the city streets. She stood and listened for a few seconds. Then, sending up a silent apology, coupled with a plea for understanding for what she was about to do, Jazmin flipped open her micro, and called her mum.

HALLY SKINNER LOOKED UP SHARPLY FROM HER LAPTOP. THE DOOR TO THE HEAD OF THE ISA'S OFFICE HAD JUST BURST OPEN, AND ASSIA HAD SHOT OUT LIKE A CORK FROM A CHAMPAGNE BOTTLE.

"Hey," Hally said, concerned by the expression on Assia's face. She half-rose in her seat. "Take it easy. What's happened?"

"It's Jazmin," Assia exclaimed. She hurried to her desk and began closing down her laptop, bundling her documents together before stuffing them haphazardly into her briefcase.

"Accident in the playground?"

"Nuh-uh." Assia shook her head vigorously. "She's found our Russian!"

Hally's mouth dropped open. "You're kidding me, right?"

Assia unplugged the laptop and placed it in the carrying case. "And guess where he turned up? At the library. Just like she said. And best of all – he's alive and well. Isn't that wonderful?"

"It's wonderful," Hally echoed dutifully.

Assia zipped the carrying case shut, slid the strap over her left shoulder and picked up her briefcase. "This whole case has suddenly turned around," she said. "I had the police report on the window cleaner this morning. Apparently he's got form. Lots of it. Armed robbery – and he always targets seniors. I can't think what that cleaning company was doing employing him. Talk about careless checking!"

"Great. So that's yet another mystery solved. And the Russian bullet?"

"Jazmin says apparently Kirilovitch has an explanation for that." Assia's face was radiant. "Sometimes my daughter truly amazes me!" she exclaimed proudly.

"Right." Hally's expression looked like she was sucking on an unripe lemon.

"Listen, I have to go," Assia said. "See you tomorrow."

Hally Skinner's eyes followed Assia as, heavily laden, she ran out of the office. For a long moment, Hally sat and stared at the gently swinging glass door. Then, her mouth set in a thin line of disapproval, she turned back to her work. That girl, Hally thought grimly. Some day, please God, she is *so not* going to land on her feet.

JAZMIN HAD JUST HANDED A MUG OF STRONG SWEET TEA TO THE OLD MAN WHEN SHE HEARD THE SOUND OF HER MUM'S KEY IN THE FRONT DOOR. THERE WAS THE THUMP OF HEAVY BAGS BEING HASTILY dropped in the hallway. Then Assia appeared in the kitchen doorway, her eyes bright and alive with relief.

"Ivan Kirilovitch, thank goodness you're safe!" she exclaimed, hurrying towards the old man, her hands outstretched. Kirilovitch shot Jazmin a silent, reproachful look. Jazmin did a shrugging palms-up and mouthed "Sorry" over her mum's shoulder. Assia enveloped him in a big hug. For a moment, there was silence. Then, glancing across the table, Jazmin noticed that Zeb was staring fixedly at her, a puzzled expression on his face, and, suddenly, she realized what had just happened.

"Ivan Kirilovitch?" Zeb said, frowning. "Who's Ivan Kirilovitch? I thought you told me this was your Great-Uncle Charles!'

AFTER THINGS HAD SETTLED DOWN ASSIA AND KIRILOVITCH HAD TALKED FOR A LONG TIME, SORTING MATTERS OUT, CLEARING THE AIR. NOW, WHILE JAZMIN AND THE OLD MAN WERE EXCHANGING Christmas memories in the lounge, Assia took her micro upstairs. She needed to have a private conversation with the head of the ISA. There were scratch marks on her peace of mind.

MEANWHILE JAZMIN SAT IN AN ARMCHAIR. HER EYES WERE OPEN, BUT HER BRAIN ELSEWHERE. AT ONE LEVEL, SHE WAS LISTENING TO THE OLD MAN'S STORIES ABOUT CHRISTMAS IN THE URALS WITH HIS wife and daughter. At a deeper level, she was revisiting the brief conversation with Zeb that she'd had earlier. Jazmin winced as she recalled how it had gone. They'd been standing together in the hallway. Zeb had said: *How come you always lie to me?* to which she'd replied: *Excuse me, exactly what lies are we talking about here?* And he'd said: *Well, first there was the lie about being new, and then there was the lie about being good at maths, and then there was the lie about playing chess, and now there's the lie about your great-uncle.* And when she'd opened her mouth to say something in her own defence, he'd held up a hand and said crossly: *Don't bother, Jazmin, because knowing you, whatever you say, it will probably only be another lie. Won't it?* And then he'd turned and walked out on her.

Jazmin heaved a great sigh. What was it with her and boys? she wondered. First Tonda, the student she'd met last summer. Now this. Just when she thought everything was sailing along smoothly, the Relationship liner hit the Crisis iceberg. Kaboom! Maybe she was doomed, she thought morosely. Maybe she was never going to have normal relationships.

Jazmin honestly didn't think she had told Zeb any lies. Not deliberately. Okay, she'd been a bit economical with the truth, but that wasn't the same thing. Anyway, as far as Kirilovitch was concerned, she'd only been following security precautions. And as for the rest, what was worse: letting Zeb think she was a genius, or acting like she fancied him rotten, like Honi had done? Honi Delacy was *majorly* untruthy. Compared with Honi, Jazmin's own multiple personality disorder coupled with a tendency to vague up things, was a mere minor social blip.

Jazmin decided she would try some saveage on the relationship because in spite of his many annoying habits she was beginning to like having Zeb Stone around as a friend. But if it didn't work, no hards. She was not going to beat herself up about it.

Having mentally sorted the latest crisis in her life, she refocused on Kirilovitch, who was well away on his memories. Jazmin glanced at the old man, feeling desperately sorry for him. Where would he spend this Christmas? she asked herself. Not on the streets. Not if she had anything to do with it. Christmas was a time for families. So maybe the old man didn't have any family he could spend the festival with right now, but hey, they could work round that. She smiled, nodded at him encouragingly and began to make plans.

ASSIA RE-ENTERED THE LIVING ROOM. TACT AND DIPLOMACY, SHE REMINDED HERSELF, OR THIS WOULD NEVER WORK. THE OLD MAN WAS STUBBORN, AND JAZMIN COULD DO OBSTINATE FOR ENGLAND.

"Everything all right?" she asked breezily.

"Fine," Jazmin replied.

Kirilovitch nodded silently.

"I thought we might have a special dinner tonight," Assia went on, smiling at him, "to celebrate your safe return."

"Nice one," Jazmin said.

Assia crossed the room and sat on the arm of the old man's chair. "Do you have any idea how worried we've all been about you, Ivan Kirilovitch?" she began quietly. "The thought of you sleeping rough on the streets in a strange country – it doesn't bear thinking about." She placed a hand over his. "I feel awful about this," she went on. "It's entirely my fault – I should have looked after you better."

"You weren't to know it would happen," the old man said, glancing up at her.

"But that doesn't change my feelings," Assia said firmly. She squeezed his hand gently. "So to show how sorry I am for what you went through, I'd like to offer you the hospitality of my home for the rest of your time in England. I'm sure it won't be for long; the ISA will find your wife and daughter – I gather from my boss that we are following some very promising leads. In the meantime, we'd both love to have you stay here with us, wouldn't we, hon?"

Assia held her breath, waiting for Jazmin's reaction. The apartment was not big, and she knew how much her daughter liked her own space and her privacy.

"Hey, *good* idea!" Jazmin grinned. *Nice one, Mum*, she thought. This was precisely the plan she'd been formulating herself. "He can have your room, can't he?" she added quickly.

"Of course he can," Assia said. She breathed a silent sigh of relief.

They both turned and looked at Kirilovitch.

"Oh, well...I..." he began hesitantly.

"Just think – you'll be able to teach me how to play chess properly," Jazmin told him, "and I could teach you how to juggle."

"Thank you so much, Ivan," Assia put in quickly, before the old man had time to voice his objections. "I really appreciate your agreeing to this, and I feel so much better now."

"I'll make up your bed right away," Jazmin said, getting up. "And after supper, we can all go and collect Tolstoy."

Damn, Assia thought. She had forgotten about the cat. "Err, well, yes, of course your cat is welcome to move in too," she lied. Assia was not an animal person.

"Hey, I finally get to have a pet!" Jazmin exclaimed. "How good is that?"

Assia cut her a long-suffering look, but Jazmin's smile was as wide as Africa.

IN THE SMALL HOURS OF THE MORNING, JAZMIN SUDDENLY SAT BOLT UPRIGHT IN BED. SHE HAD BEEN WOKEN UP BY A MYSTERIOUS SCRATCHING NOISE JUST OUTSIDE HER BEDROOM DOOR. SHE remained totally still, every muscle and fibre of her body taut. Burglars? she thought. She listened hard. The noise seemed to be coming from somewhere low down, near the floor. Burglars with restricted growth problems? Jazmin slid from under the duvet, tiptoed across the carpet and opened the door a crack.

The black and white cat was sitting outside on the landing. It miaowed a friendly greeting before pushing its way in. "Oh, it's you," Jazmin whispered, feeling relieved. She went back to bed. The cat followed. It jumped lightly on the bed and curled itself closely into the small of her back, purring loudly. "Bet you're not allowed to do this at home," she told it, pulling up her duvet.

Jazmin settled herself down. Everything had worked out just right, she thought to herself happily. Her mum was now sleeping downstairs on the sofa, the old guy (and his gun) had taken up temporary occupancy of her mum's room, and she had been invaded by a cat that did motorbike impressions. But she could live with that. If only every problem was as easy to sort, she thought ruefully, her life would be just peachy. And the reason it wasn't was because the Chaos Fairy was always just a bit better organized than she was.

NEXT MORNING, JAZMIN GOT UP EARLY WHILE THE APARTMENT WAS STILL QUIET. IT WAS TIME TO FULFIL HER LONG-STANDING, BUT FREQUENTLY BROKEN RESOLUTION: SHE WAS GOING TO EXERCISE. Exercise gave you endorphins. Jazmin wasn't totally sure what they were, but she knew they were a good thing. She stuffed herself into a tracksuit and an old long-sleeved vest, did some stretches, then headed out into the cold, grey morning.

By the time Jazmin returned the apartment had come to life. Bacon smells mixed with the fragrant aroma of fresh coffee came wafting out from the kitchen. Classical music was filtering down from upstairs. Scarlet-faced and panting, Jazmin did some hasty warm-downs in the hall, then followed her nose.

Her mum turned round from the cooker. "You've been out running, hon? I'm very impressed," she said admiringly.

Jazmin smirked.

Her mum paused. She peered at her, eyes narrowing. "Looks like you've got icing sugar on your top."

Jazmin shrugged. "Must've fallen out of the sky."

"I see." Assia turned back to her cooking with a knowing smile.

Jazmin pretended she hadn't noticed. She sat down at

the table and reached for the juice. Next time she ran past the baker's, she'd try not to stop, she promised herself. Even if the cake order was being delivered.

Her mum placed a plate of bacon and eggs in front of her. "That cat keeps trying to lick the butter," she complained.

"Awww, he's only making himself at home," Jazmin said.

Assia pursed her lips. "So what are your plans for today?"

Jazmin dipped a forkful of crispy bacon into the egg yolk. "I'm going Christmas shopping," she announced.

"Good for you."

"Only..." Jazmin drawled, looking up hopefully.

"Why do I know what's coming?"

"I could use a loan. Just a small one. If that's all right?"

Assia shook her head disapprovingly, but she was smiling. "Where does your money go?"

"Yeah, mystery," Jazmin agreed. "It's like: money talks – mine says goodbye."

Assia pulled the frying pan off the heat and reached for her bag. "Actually I don't mind lending you some money. You did an excellent job finding Ivan," she said, unzipping her purse. "Is this enough?"

Jazmin pocketed the crisp notes. "That'll do nicely," she said.

There was the sound of heavy footsteps going slowly along the landing.

"Sounds like the bathroom's free," Assia said.

Jazmin glanced towards the half-open kitchen door. "What's going to happen to him now?" she asked.

"Today, he's coming with me," Assia said. "My boss wants to talk to him. And we've got a conference call with our Russian team. They need to talk to him too."

Jazmin picked up her empty plate and put it in the dishwasher. "I meant now as in the future," she said.

"Well, we're gradually tracking down everybody linked to Boris Arkady," Assia said. "We also still want to interview his son, Nikolai, of course – the New York guys have assigned some serious manpower to search for him. As soon as Stash and Suki find Kirilovitch's wife and daughter, he'll give us the tape."

"And then?"

Assia considered this. "And then, hopefully, we can somehow get them back together again."

"I so hope they can find them," Jazmin said. "It'd be great to get him back with his family after all this time apart. Hey, wouldn't it be amazing if we could reunite them for Christmas?" She smiled.

Assia pursed her mouth. It was not going to be as easy as that, she thought. And yet... Miracles could happen sometimes, couldn't they? "I'm keeping my fingers crossed," she said.

It FELT PRETTY GENIUS TO BE WALKING TO THE MALL ON A COLD BRIGHT DAY WITH LOTS OF MONEY IN HER POCKET, JAZMIN THOUGHT TO HERSELF. ESPECIALLY WHEN IT WAS MONEY SHE'D EARNED legitimately. *Jaz Dawson, sassy superheroine, always got her man.* Feeling strong and empowery, Jazmin took out her micro. Now was the perfect time to do some damage limitation on her relationship with Zeb, she decided. She flipped the micro open and texted him a message.

Several long hours later, Jazmin Dawson sat exhausted on a bench by the indoor skating rink. It was strange how shopping was so much better in anticipation than in reality. Equally strange was how she always forgot this important fact. Nevertheless, she consoled herself as she gently flexed her aching feet, she had had a really successful morning. Okay, her paycard was maxed, and she'd blown all the money her mum'd given her, but she'd got Christmas sorted for another year.

Jazmin glanced smugly sideways at the bright gift bags on the bench beside her. She had bought a whole bunch of great presents, she thought. And she'd also seen some clothes she might buy for herself when she got her Christmas money from her rich uncle and aunt. Best of all, by the time she hit the mall to buy them, she'd probably be a whole size smaller, thanks to all the exercise she was planning to do over the holiday. Not that she was fat, she reminded herself, just a bit short for her weight. She rose to her feet, collected her bags and set off home.

DOWNSTAIRS IN THE APARTMENT KITCHEN, JAZMIN DISCOVERED THE OLD MAN'S BLACK AND WHITE CAT CROUCHED ON THE TABLE. IT WAS STARING AT THE FRIDGE DOOR, AS IF WILLING IT TO OPEN. SHE shooed it off the table. The cat gave her an indignant look and went to sit by its bowl. "You are such a gutzo," she told it disapprovingly, pouring out some cat biscuits. She made herself a cheese and pickle sandwich, and went back up to her room. All that shopping had tired her out. An afternoon curled up with one of her exciting new books was beckoning.

Several hours later, Jazmin heard the front door opening. Her mum and the old guy were back. She struggled into a sitting position, listening to their voices in the hallway. The old man sounded as if he were cross about something. She heard his footsteps stomping up the stairs. Then the door to his room slammed shut. Uh-oh, she thought. Her secret-agency sense was detecting a bad case of the suspicious. Something had gone wrong.

Jazmin put down her book and crept out onto the landing. Loud classical music was now coming from the old man's room. She tiptoed downstairs and discovered her mum seated at her desk in the corner of the lounge. She was drumming her fingers on the shiny rosewood surface and staring straight ahead. Not a good sign. As Jazmin entered the room her mum gave her a brief smile. "Well, that didn't go quite as well as I expected," she remarked drily.

"Tell me." Jazmin perched on the arm of a chair.

Assia expelled air. "Unh. Where do I start?" she sighed. "I'm afraid our Russian agents gave Ivan rather a hard time. Understandable, I suppose – they've been putting in long hours on this case, and now just when it's finally coming together they're suddenly told about a vital new piece of evidence. But they're not allowed to see it."

"We're talking about the file he copied?"

"Uh-huh," Assia nodded. "And the trouble is, we only have his word that it exists in the first place. Our I.T. people have taken Arkady's computer to bits again to try to find the original document. And once again, they've found nothing."

"But you believe him, don't you?"

"Yes, I do," Assia said. "But it seems I'm in a minority of one. Our Russian team clearly think he's fabricated the whole thing to get us to find his family. They say that we already have a good enough case against Boris Arkady. They even went so far as to suggest to my boss that there are more important things Stash and Suki could be doing."

"But that's terrible!" Jazmin exclaimed. "He needs to get back with his wife and daughter."

"Tell me about it." Assia pulled a face. "The whole thing is a total nightmare. If my boss decides to bring Stash and Suki out of Russia, we'll never find Ivan's family. Which means we'll never get our hands on the file. There's a distinct possibility that everything I've worked so hard to set up is about to collapse like a house of cards."

She rested her chin in her hands. "Oh dear," she sighed. "Poor old man. I seem to have let him down yet again."

Jazmin gave her mum a supportive hug. "No you haven't," she said. "He trusts you. He likes you."

Assia shook her head. "Not right now. I've never seen him so angry. There was a lot of shouting in Russian. At one point, he started banging on the desk with his fist."

"So why doesn't he prove them all wrong?" Jazmin suggested. "He could just give you the file. Then they'd have to believe him."

Assia sighed. "You think I haven't tried that one?" she said. "I've begged and pleaded. All the way back in the taxi. The way he sees it, the file is his only security. And he's not going to part with it until he gets what he wants. We've reached a total impasse," Assia said, pulling a wry face, "and the worst of it is, I simply don't have a clue what to do next."

Jazmin eased herself off the arm of her chair. "Hey, maybe some tea would help to calm things down," she suggested. "I'll go put the kettle on, shall I?"

Assia expelled air. "Thanks, hon," she said, trying to force a smile. "That's really nice of you. I'm sure Ivan would appreciate something to drink. Unfortunately, long term I think it's going to take a bit more than a cup of tea to sort all of this out."

UPSTAIRS, THE OLD MAN WAS SITTING ON THE EDGE OF THE BED. SO MUCH OF HIS LIFE HAD BEEN SPENT SITTING ON HIS OWN IN PLACES THAT WERE NOT HIS, HE THOUGHT SADLY TO HIMSELF. CHEAP HOTEL rooms, berths on ships. Even the small flatlet in the sixteenth *arrondissement* of Paris, where he'd lived for so long, never really felt like home. Home was where your family was. This was a home, but once again, it was not his. Kirilovitch sat motionless, remembering his family. Sometimes he felt that keeping memories in his head was like having a knife in his pocket. Each time he remembered, it cut him and he bled.

On the other side of the window, the afternoon sky was winter white. Gusts of wind tore the last dying leaves off the trees and tossed them into the air. The old man sat and watched the leaves performing their final dance of death, but he did not really see them. Transfixed by the bright knife of memory, his mind had drawn him back into that world that was more real to him than the one outside his window.

ASSIA TIPPED THE LEFTOVERS INTO THE RECYCLING BIN AT THE BACK OF THE APARTMENT BLOCK. THE RUSSIAN HAD BARELY TOUCHED HIS DINNER, SHE REFLECTED SADLY. THE MEETING HAD clearly affected him even more deeply than she had realized. Old wounds had been reopened, new hopes dashed. Assia shook her head. And it wasn't just him. Jazmin, who could normally dine for England, had merely picked at her lamb moussaka and had declined a second helping of treacle tart.

Assia hadn't appreciated how the old man had become absorbed into the fabric of both their lives. After eating in total silence, Jazmin and Kirilovitch had both got up from the table and drifted into the living room, where they'd ended up sitting opposite each other, still hardly speaking. Which was why, after loading the dishwasher, Assia had decided to go and sort the rubbish out. She needed to get some air and clear her thoughts.

Walking back to the apartment, Assia tried to focus on the positive. Maybe events were currently conspiring against her, but that could always change. It wasn't over until it was over. Opening the front door, she was met by Jazmin coming out of the living room. To Assia's relief her daughter was looking much more cheerful. "My friend Zeb's just called. Is it all right if he comes round?" she asked.

"Sure," Assia nodded. Maybe a fresh face might cheer the Russian up a bit too, she thought.

"We're going to have a chess tournament," Jazmin told her, adding: "Well, they are. I'm going to watch and learn."

Assia peered over her daughter's shoulder. In the living room, Kirilovitch was carefully setting up his chessboard on the coffee table. A cursory glance showed that he looked considerably happier too. In addition, she also noticed that Tchaikovsky's *1812 Overture* was thumping out of the music centre. A triumphant piece celebrating a Russian victory over great suffering. She guessed he had chosen it, and why.

Her thoughts suddenly clear, Assia went and got her micro from her briefcase. Then she took it quietly into the kitchen and closed the door behind her. She had an important call to make. To two people who were on a special mission somewhere in Russia. What she could do, she would. And what she could do was to make sure that the search for the old man's wife and child was not called off. Not just yet.

JAZMIN STARED IN PUZZLED FASCINATION AT HER BREAKFAST BOWL OF MUESLI. WHY WAS MUESLI SO WEIRD? WHY, IN THE FACE OF ALL SCIENTIFIC LOGIC, DID THE BIG BRAZIL NUTS REFUSE TO SINK TO THE bottom of the bowl? It was a constant mystery. There was gravity, and then there was muesli.

"I'm just going to take Ivan up a cup of tea," her mum said, derailing her train of thought.

Jazmin stopped poking the Brazil nuts around with her spoon. "I was thinking," she said, "maybe Zeb and I could be his bodyguards."

Assia threw up a mental image of this suggestion. "I don't think so."

Jazmin pulled a disappointed face. Darn. She had already worked out a whole bunch of exciting scenarios in which Jaz Dawson, her tall, glamorous crime-fighting alter-ego rescued old men from Evil Russians and did a bit of world saveage on the side.

"But someone needs to keep an eye on him," she insisted. "We can't just let him wander around on his own."

"Don't worry," Assia told her, "I have no intention of letting him out of my sight. Actually, I'm just waiting for a courier to bring round a personal tracking unit for him. Then we'll make some plans for the day."

"Oh yeah – what sort of plans?" Jazmin asked.

"I'm sure I can come up with something interesting to do," Assia said. "Which reminds me," she added, "that cat has knocked several baubles off the Christmas tree."

"Aww, he's only playing," Jazmin said.

Assia rolled her eyes and left the kitchen, carrying the cup of tea.

NIKOLAI ARKADY WAS ENJOYING A LATE BREAKFAST IN HIS EXPENSIVE MAYFAIR HOTEL ROOM. HE SIPPED HIS BITTER, BLACK FILTERED COFFEE AND LOOKED OUT OVER THE ROOFTOPS OF London. The thick glass of the double-glazed window cut to a far-distant murmur the noise of traffic passing below.

It seemed like a pleasant winter day out there, Nikolai thought to himself. He split open a freshly baked croissant and spread it thickly with Irish butter. When he finished his breakfast, he would take a shower, and then go out. He had one more important thing to do before flying back to Russia.

After all, he had a wife and kids waiting for his return. And it was nearly Christmas.

JAZMIN STOOD ABSOLUTELY STILL, GAZING HYPNOTICALLY UPWARDS. ORNATE GILT-TOPPED BANISTER RAILS AND PALE MARBLE PILLARS STRETCHED UP TO A WHITE AND GOLD PAINTED ceiling. Light drifted down from the central glass ceiling panel and from long bunches of halogen tubes which hung over the deep stairwell on thin silver wires. Extreme wow-factor, she thought.

"Hey, hon," Assia said, grabbing her arm and shaking her out of her trance. "Don't just stand there; you're causing a traffic jam. We're going to look at the gifts now – I think we can cut through the men's department. Come on, this way."

Jazmin trailed slowly after her mum and Kirilovitch. This was such a good idea, she thought. She'd never been to Harrods before, although she'd gone past the big, expensive Knightsbridge department store many times on her way to one of the London museums. She cut a quick glance at her mum, who had taken Kirilovitch's arm, and was gently steering him through the throng of well-dressed

Christmas shoppers. It had been her idea to spend the morning in Harrods looking around. Jazmin silently congratulated her. This place was amazing. She was having the best time. And the old man looked as if he was enjoying himself too.

THE SMARTLY SUITED ASSISTANT IN THE MEN'S DEPARTMENT LIKED HIS JOB. ESPECIALLY AROUND CHRISTMAS, WHICH WAS A PEAK SELLING PERIOD. SHIRTS, TIES, SWEATERS, SOCKS, BOXES OF linen handkerchiefs and cufflinks just seemed to walk out of the store, such was the demand for presents. People liked to spend extravagantly at Christmas. The customer he was serving now was no exception. A foreign gentleman, casually but expensively dressed in a navy cashmere sweater, dark wool trousers and a soft chocolate-brown leather jacket. He was buying as if money was no object.

Already a pile of shirts, butter-yellow, sky-blue and palest sea-green, lay strewn casually on the counter like a pastel rainbow. The assistant noted with approval that the customer had selected only the very best English labels: Turnbull & Asser and Thomas Pink. Italian silk ties snaked their brightly striped and spotted way over and around the shirts. The customer handed over his American Express Gold paycard to the assistant.

"I'd like all these things wrapped and delivered as soon as possible," he commanded, giving the man a small card which bore the name and address of a very expensive Mayfair hotel.

"Certainly, sir," the assistant responded. "I'll make sure it is dealt with immediately."

The assistant busied himself at the till. When he turned back, however, he noticed a strange and unaccountable change had suddenly come over his customer. The man's formerly pleasant smile had vanished. The colour had drained out of his face. His whole body stance was rigid, and he was staring intently at something on the other side of the department.

Intrigued, the assistant followed the man's gaze, but he couldn't see anything unusual. Just a nondescript woman with short mousy hair, accompanied by a teenage girl and an elderly man. They were making their way towards the gift department.

NIKOLAI ARKADY FOLLOWED THE WOMAN, EVEN THOUGH THE LOGICAL SIDE OF HIS BRAIN TOLD HIM HE MUST BE MISTAKEN. THE WOMAN AND THE GIRL WERE COMPLETE STRANGERS. THE OLD MAN with them was not Kirilovitch. It could not be. Kirilovitch was dead. He'd paid people to take care of it. And yet the likeness was uncanny. Keeping just a few feet away, Nikolai tracked the little group until they came to a halt in front of a display of luxury chess sets.

With catlike tread, Nikolai drew nearer. He had to be sure

in his own mind that the resemblance of this man to his hated brother-in-law, the one man on the planet who had it in his power to ruin his beloved father, was nothing more than mere coincidence. A trick of the light. He placed himself behind a table of expensive Hermès leather goods and pretended to examine them. From this secluded vantage point, he could hear what was being said without being seen.

The teenage girl was bending down, looking at one of the chess sets.

"Hey, nice horses," he heard her say.

"Knights," the woman corrected her.

"I like these glass ones," the girl went on, picking up one of the pieces. "Prawn to d4," she intoned solemnly.

The woman clicked her teeth, and shook her head. "I don't think you're meant to touch things," she said, replacing the pawn back on its original square.

"Whoa – this set is seriously expensive!" the girl exclaimed. "Hey, Mum, who has this sort of money?"

"Seriously rich people," the woman told her.

The girl turned to the old man. "Could you have afforded this?" she asked him. "You were rich once, weren't you?"

The old man smiled indulgently at her. "Once upon a time," he said, "but that was a very long time ago."

Nikolai Arkady felt an icy-cold finger run lightly along his spine. That voice. He'd know it anywhere. Cautiously, he raised his head and subjected the old guy to a long, searching glance. Once again you were meant to be dead, old man, he thought silently, his eyes narrowing, and once again you are alive.

Nikolai's hand slipped to the inside pocket of his leather jacket. The old man had cheated death so many times, it was almost as if he and Fate were playing some macabre game against each other. But every game must ultimately come to an end, Nikolai thought grimly, his fingers tightening around something in his pocket. And now it was time to finish this game, once and for all.

Nikolai pursued the little group into the food hall. He watched while the woman bought a small canister of tea in the green and gold Harrods store colours. "An early Christmas present for you," she said gaily, handing it to the old man, and Nikolai smiled to himself, thinking of the present that he too was shortly to deliver. But not here, not yet, he decided. There were too many people; it was too public. Instead, he forced himself to focus his attention, albeit temporarily, upon a display of luscious hand-made chocolates.

Biding his time, like a snake in the shadow of a rock, Nikolai Arkady waited patiently for the right opportunity to strike.

HER NOSE TWITCHING LIKE A DOG WHO'D SMELLED A RABBIT, JAZMIN STROLLED ROUND THE FOOD HALL. SHE WAS IN FOODIE HEAVEN. SHE WANDERED FROM COUNTER TO COUNTER, HER EYES alight with interest, gazing at all the eaty stuff. This would be a majorly wonderful place to get a Saturday job, she told herself, her mind racing ahead to all the tasting opportunities. Suddenly, her face lit up. "Hey, Mum – look over there – they do Krispy Kreme doughnuts," she breathed.

Assia's eyes followed her pointing finger. "So they do."

"We could buy a box of them to take back with us," Jazmin suggested, assuming a last-puppy-in-the-pet-shop expression.

Assia laughed good-humouredly. "Go on then," she said, fishing out her purse. "You choose what you want. We'll wait for you in the fruit and vegetable section." She slipped her arm through Kirilovitch's. "You have to see the peacock mosaics they have on the walls in there," she told him, "they're quite wonderful."

STILL SHADOWED BY HIS HIDDEN ENEMY, THE OLD MAN STROLLED INTO THE NEXT SECTION OF THE FOOD HALL, ARM IN ARM WITH ASSIA. THEY LOOKED AROUND FOR A WHILE, ADMIRING THE decorated walls and ceilings, commenting upon the heaped up piles of jewel-bright exotic fruit. Then Assia bought a pineapple, the old man confessing that he hadn't tasted one for over ten years. After a brief stroll around, they were rejoined by Jazmin, who was carrying a white cardboard box.

Jazmin breathed in deeply. "Smells gorgeous in here," she said. "Where now?"

"I thought we'd find somewhere to have coffee and cake," Assia suggested.

"Good idea," Jazmin agreed. "Looking at all this food's making me hungry."

"This is all very kind of you," Kirilovitch said with a wistful sigh. "I hardly feel I deserve such a treat after everything that's happened."

"Nonsense," Assia cut in, "of course you deserve a treat. We all do." She studied her store plan. "There seems to be a café on the second floor," she said. "Come on, I think the escalators are through here."

Nikolai Arkady sat in an alcove at a single table, a copy of a daily newspaper open in front of him. From his secluded vantage point he watched the old man and his friends tucking into fresh scones with jam and clotted cream. Pretending to be engrossed in his paper, Nikolai sipped the dark filter coffee he habitually drank and contemplated his next move.

Suddenly, the little group finished their food. The teenager and the old man got up to leave. The woman went to queue at the cash desk. Nikolai thrust some coins at one of the waitresses to pay for his coffee. Then, holding his paper in front of him like a shield, he drifted out of the restaurant and set off once more in pursuit of his quarry. His dark leather brogues barely made any sound on the highly polished woodblock floor. He followed them through the kitchen department and into the books and magazines section.

Ah yes, books, Nikolai thought scornfully. He remembered Ivan Kirilovitch's great love affair with the written word. His house on the outskirts of Ekaterinburg used to be full of books, piled up on every stair, overflowing from every shelf. He himself had no particular love for books. There was no money to be made from them. Books were a waste of time. Why read, when you could be out making money? That was his opinion.

JAZMIN SCANNED THE BOOKSHELVES, HER EYES GLEAMING. "WHOA – LOOK AT ALL THESE GREAT BOOKS," SHE BREATHED. SHE REACHED UP, LIFTED ONE DOWN AND BEGAN READING THE BIT ON the back cover.

The old man touched her lightly on the shoulder. "I'm just going to..." he said quietly, nodding in the direction of the men's toilets.

"Right," Jazmin said.

Kirilovitch turned and walked towards the cloakroom

door. A few seconds later, Jazmin's peripheral vision picked up a man in a chocolate-brown leather jacket heading in the same direction.

ASSIA CAUGHT UP WITH JAZMIN IN THE TRAVEL SECTION OF THE BOOK DEPARTMENT, WHERE SHE WAS WORKING HER WAY THROUGH A LAVISH DISPLAY OF PICTURE BOOKS ON LONDON.

"I thought I'd buy one of these books for Ivan," Jazmin said, "it would remind him of his stay here with us."

Assia nodded approvingly. "Good idea, hon."

Jazmin sighed, assuming an expression of pre-emptive meekness. "Well, I *would* buy him a book, only..." She hesitated, cutting her eyes at her mum.

"Don't tell me..." Assia groaned. She reached for her purse.

"Thanks, Mum, you're the best." Jazmin grinned. "I think I'll get him this one; it's got lots of good pictures."

Assia glanced round the department. "Where is he, by the way? I can't see him anywhere."

"He's just gone to the toilets," Jazmin told her. "He'll be back in a minute." She tucked the book under her arm, and went over to the pay desk. Assia watched her walking away. She glanced round the department, a frown gathering between her eyebrows as the seconds ticked by, and the old man failed to reappear.

WHILE JAZMIN STOOD IN THE QUEUE WAITING TO PAY FOR HER BOOK, ASSIA CONTINUED SCOPING OUT THE DEPARTMENT, A WORRIED EXPRESSION ON HER FACE. WHERE WAS IVAN Kirilovitch? It didn't take that long to visit the men's cloakroom. She hoped he hadn't got lost; Harrods was a big store. There were lots of walkways, all looking the same. She checked her watch again, then stood drumming her fingers on the back of her hand.

"Hey, Mum, did you see that man in the leather jacket who just ran along the walkway?" Jazmin exclaimed, hurrying over. "He was really rude – he barged straight into me and nearly knocked me over. No apology or anything."

But Assia wasn't listening. Her attention had been caught by a couple of shop assistants hurrying purposefully towards the far end of the book department.

"Isn't that where the men's cloakroom is?" she asked, pointing.

Jazmin nodded quickly.

Assia looked around. "Where's Ivan?"

"I don't know. Hasn't he come back yet?"

For a split second, Assia and Jazmin stood motionless, each reading the dawning realization in the other's eyes. Then Assia broke free. "Come on!" she cried. She turned and ran in the same direction as the hurrying crowd of shoppers. Jazmin hustled after her. Please, she prayed, please let nothing terrible have happened to him.

A CROWD OF CUSTOMERS WAS GATHERiNG OUTSIDE THE MEN'S CLOAKROOM AS WORD QUiCKLY GOT ROUND THAT SOMETHiNG iMPORTANT HAD OCCURRED. ASSiA UNCEREMONiOUSLY ELBOWED her way to the front, where a trio of male assistants were nervously guarding the entrance.

"What's happened?" she asked.

"Nothing to worry about, madam," one of the assistants informed her in a soothing voice.

"Nothing to *worry* about?" a smartly dressed woman in the crowd exclaimed indignantly. "Somebody's been STABBED! In Harrods! In broad daylight! What on *earth* is the world coming to?"

Assia reached into her pocket and pulled out her ID card. She stepped forward and waved it in the assistant's face. "ISA," she stated loudly and clearly. "Please let me pass."

The assistant gave the card a quick glance. He took a step to one side and let her through. Then he stepped back and with a self-important air, refolded his arms before taking up his former position in front of the door. Jazmin did a face-scrunch. She so needed to go where her mum had just gone. She hunted around in her purse until she found her library card. It was white and carried her photo, and was almost, but not quite, identical to her mum's ID card, so long as you didn't examine it too closely.

"ISA," she said, flashing the library card briefly in front of the assistant's eyes with vision-blurring speed. She jerked her thumb forward. "I'm with her, right?"

Quickly palming the card, Jazmin ducked under his arm and hustled through the door to the men's cloakroom before the bewildered assistant had time to react.

ON THE OTHER SIDE OF THE DOOR, THE CLOAKROOM STAFF WERE STANDING BY THE MARBLE BASINS, THEIR FACES BLANCHED AND APPREHENSIVE. KIRILOVITCH WAS LYING ON HIS BACK UPON THE black and white tiled floor. A male customer was crouched next to him, pushing down on the old man's chest. He glanced up briefly when first Assia, closely followed by Jazmin, appeared, then calmly got on with what he was doing. Assia ducked down next to him, her eyes fixed on Kirilovitch's face. "Do you want me to take over?" she asked quietly.

The man shook his head. "They've called an ambulance," he told her.

"Right. I'll check it's on its way and hurry it along," Assia said. She hauled out her micro and began dialling.

"But...but..." Jazmin stammered. She stared down, aghast. Kirilovitch's skin was as white as the marble tiles upon which his head lay. His eyes were shut. His lips were blue. Blood was seeping ominously through the right side of his jacket.

The man placed his ear on Kirilovitch's chest and listened. He covered the old man's nose, lifted his chin and breathed quickly into his mouth twice.

"Is he all right?" Jazmin faltered, realizing even as she spoke, that this would be a winning entry in a Really Stupid Things To Say contest.

"I think he's had a heart attack." The man interlocked his fingers and started pushing firmly and rhythmically down upon the right side of the old man's chest. "One...two...three..." he counted out loud.

And the blood? Jazmin thought. Why aren't you saying about the blood? Horrified, she stared at the familiar frayed tweed jacket, at the bright crimson drops splattered on the floor and felt her head swim, her gorge rising. She had never seen a dead body before, but even to her amateur eyes, the old man looked awfully dead.

"Thirteen...fourteen...fifteen," the man said. He quickly breathed twice into the old guy's mouth, then resumed the pushing and counting again.

There was a sudden flurry of activity at the door.

"The paramedics are here," Assia said. She bent over and gently brushed a lock of the old man's hair from his forehead. "Don't die on me, Ivan Kirilovitch," she whispered softly into his ear. "Not now. Not when we're so near to finding your family."

JAZMIN WAS SITTING AT HER MUM'S DESK IN THE ISA BUILDING. SHE WAS MAKING A VERY LONG PAPER-CLIP CHAIN. MAJOR DISPLACEMENT ACTIVITY. EVERY FEW SECONDS HER EYES FLICKED across the office to the closed door at the far end. On the other side of that door was the head of the ISA's office. Her mum and a senior police officer were in there, along with the head of the ISA.

Eventually, the door to the office opened and her mum reappeared. Jazmin glanced anxiously up at her. Assia hurried straight over and put an arm round her shoulders. "Well, the police have issued a red alert to all ports, airports and terminals," she said. "Mr. Nikolai Arkady won't get away from us this time."

"So that man who ran into me – it was him?" Jazmin asked.

"We're almost certain it was. Either that, or he has an identical twin."

"Whoa – he was here in London all the time, not New York."

Assia nodded grimly. The question of how Nikolai Arkady managed to get in under the radar was one she'd eventually have to find answers to. But not right now.

"Well done for being able to describe him so accurately," she said. "That was very impressive."

Jazmin tried, and failed, to look modest.

Assia checked her watch. "My boss says we can go now," she said, "so I thought you might like an early dinner. There's a pizzeria just round the corner. I think you deserve a treat after everything that's happened."

"Okay," Jazmin nodded. She was starving. Being a superhero certainly gave you an appetite.

"And then later, we can call in at the hospital and check how things are going."

"For sure." Jazmin dropped her paper-clip chain in her mother's in-tray, and stood up ready to go.

She followed her mum into the lift, and pressed the button for the ground floor.

THE OLD MAN OPENED HIS EYES. ONCE AGAIN, HE WAS LYING ON HIS BACK IN A BED. IT WAS NOT HIS OWN BED. AT THE FOOT OF THE BED, A YOUNG GIRL IN A BLACK JUMPER WAS SITTING ON A RED plastic chair. Her dark hair was tied back in a messy ponytail. She was staring at him intently, a worried expression on her face, but as his eyes met hers her features broke into a smile.

"Hi," Jazmin said. "Welcome back."

Kirilovitch's brain threw up random puzzle pieces from the past eight hours, which it then proceeded to reassemble into a cohesive narrative.

"Ah," he winced, as the memory returned.

"You are a legend," Jazmin told him admiringly. "I've never met anybody who's nearly been killed quite as often as you."

The corners of the old guy's mouth twitched imperceptibly. "Thanks," he muttered. "I think!"

Jazmin leaned forward on her chair. "Hey, you're going to be fine," she said. "They've done some complicated heart thingy. Mum's just checking it out with the doctor."

Kirilovitch closed his eyes. "Good," he murmured.

Jazmin waited for a bit, but the old man's eyes did not reopen. She sat on, watching the thin luminous line on the heart monitor as it pulsed across the screen. After a while, Assia came quietly into the room.

Jazmin whispered: "He knew who I was."

"Of course I knew who you were," the old man growled, opening his eyes again.

Pulling up a second chair close to the bed, Assia sat down. "How are you feeling?" she asked him.

"Sore," he replied plaintively.

"It's to be expected: you've had an operation," Assia said. "But it could have been so much worse; you might very easily have died." She reached across the bed, took a very small object off his locker and laid it on top of the blanket. "I don't know why you had this particular icon in your breast pocket, but the doctor told me that it stopped the knife fatally piercing your lung."

The old man looked at the tiny icon. "I've always carried it with me ever since I left Russia. It was my mother's favourite icon; she prayed to it every day," he said.

The faces of the woman and the child stared out calmly

and peacefully. The woman smiled seraphically. The child's right hand was raised in silent blessing. Light radiated in a circle from his head. But in his tiny side there was a great gash, as if somebody had stabbed him with a spear.

"Hey – look at that: Baby Jesus saved your life," Jazmin said with a grin.

Kirilovitch inhaled sharply. He stretched out a trembling hand and picked up the icon. His eyes closed, and his lips began to move, as if he was having a silent conversation with some unseen visitor at his bedside. Then he looked up at Assia. "'Greater love has no one than this, that he lay down his life for his friends,'" he said quietly. He turned the icon over, broke off a piece of its wooden back and tipped a small silver key into the palm of his hand. Silently, he offered the key to Assia.

"Go to the Banque de France in the Rue Croix des Petits Champs, in Paris," he told her, his voice shaking with emotion. "Ask for the safe deposit box belonging to Monsieur Jean Brun. This is the key to open it. Inside, you will find a memory stick. It contains the file from the Arkadia Clinic."

Assia stared down at him. "Why?" she said, wonderingly. "Why now, after all this time?"

The old man's cheeks were suddenly wet with tears. He wiped his streaming eyes on his sleeve, his face monstrous with sorrow. "Because I lived with the icon all my life, but only now do I realize what it is saying." He handed her the key. "Make the world a better place, Assia," he said. Then, slowly, painfully, he rolled over onto his side, and turned his face to the wall.

NEXT MORNING, ZEB STONE WAS PLAYING CYBER-CHESS IN HIS BEDROOM WHEN HIS MICRO WENT OFF. THE GAME, WHICH HAD BEEN GOING ON FOR A LONG TIME, HAD REACHED A STRATEGICALLY critical point, and he was waiting for his unseen opponent to make his next move. Zeb checked the caller ID. It was Jazmin. He picked up the micro.

"Hey!" Jazmin said cheerfully. "Are you doing anything important?"

"Well...I..."

"Great. Because I have some amazing stuff to tell you!"

Jazmin began to describe in graphic detail what had happened on her visit to Harrods. Zeb listened in an astonished silence until she had talked herself to a standstill. "Whoa – things certainly happen to you, don't they?" he said, impressed.

"Yup," Jazmin agreed happily.

"How is the old man?" Zeb asked.

"He's getting better. I'm going to visit him this afternoon. Want to come?"

"Sure," Zeb said. There was a pause. "Shame they didn't catch Arkady," he remarked.

"But they did," Jazmin told him. "Didn't I mention

that? They got him late yesterday night. The police intercepted him at Heathrow trying to board a flight for Moscow. He was using a false passport. Of course, as soon as I saw him in the book department, I knew he was a criminal."

"Really?"

"Oh yeah," Jazmin said breezily. "I can pick them out instantly. It's my spidey-sense. It's never wrong."

"I see."

They talked some more until eventually Jazmin rang off, and Zeb returned to his chess game once more. He studied the board for a while, noting his opponent's move. Then with a satisfied sigh, he moved his queen into position.

Checkmate, he typed. *Game over.*

THE PARiS-LONDON SUPERSPEED TRAiN PULLED iNTO ST. PANCRAS STATiON. ASSiA ALiGHTED, WALKED THROUGH THE BARRiER AND TOOK A CAB STRAiGHT TO THE iSA HEADQUARTERS. iN HER BAG, safely zipped in a side pocket, was a small padded envelope containing the memory stick. As soon as she arrived, she went straight to the conference room, where the head of the ISA and the two Russian agents were waiting. Assia handed over the memory stick. The head of the ISA inserted it into the USB port.

LATER THAT MORNING, ASSIA HAD A FINAL DEBRIEFING WITH HER BOSS. THE HEAD OF THE ISA WAS IN A JUBILANT MOOD. "I'VE ALREADY HAD REQUESTS FROM INTERPOL, THE FSB AND THE FBI," HE told her. "They'd all like to view Kirilovitch's file as soon as possible. And that's before the various medical authorities get their hands on it. It appears that Arkady was using a worldwide network of private clinics and hospitals to source the organs he needed for all his operations."

"And the face transplants?" Assia said. "How was he sourcing them? Do you think he was arranging for people to be killed to order?"

"I fear so. There's no other way he could have done it. The man is a monster; the world is a better place without him free in it." The head of the ISA paused. "I visited Kirilovitch in hospital last night, told him how grateful the ISA was that he finally changed his mind and decided to co-operate with us after all."

Assia murmured something non-committal. She had not told her boss exactly how the old man had reached his decision to hand over the file. It was not her story to tell.

"Any word from Smith and McGregor?"

Assia did a palms-up. "Last time I heard, they were heading north," she told him.

The head of the ISA frowned. "Russia is such an immense country," he remarked. "I guess it's very easy to lose yourself in it." He looked at her. "Smith and McGregor are two of our best Field Agents," he said evenly. "And however grateful we are, I'm afraid we can't keep them on this indefinitely. I've already had a call from our colleagues in Madrid – they're investigating a counterfeiting racket, and they want to bring Smith and McGregor in on the team."

Assia sighed, biting back the feeling of disappointment. She'd really hoped the old man's wife and daughter would have been found by now.

"Maybe if Kirilovitch decides to go back to Russia he could look for them himself," the head of the ISA suggested. "Naturally, we'll provide whatever initial protection he feels he needs."

Assia said nothing. This was not the outcome she wanted.

The head of the ISA sat back in his seat, folding his arms behind his head. He cut Assia a look, as if he knew exactly what she was thinking. "This has been a difficult assignment, Agent Dawson," he said quietly. "Tough on you especially, eh? But at the end of the day, the most important thing is that we got enough evidence to close down the Arkadia Clinic for ever and put Boris Arkady and his son away for a long time."

SOME TIME LATER, A RATHER REFLECTIVE ASSIA RETURNED TO HER DESK. USUALLY SHE EXPERIENCED A FEELING OF ELATION WHEN A CASE WAS SUCCESSFULLY COMPLETED. RIGHT NOW, she felt empty.

Try as she might, she kept recalling the expression on Kirilovitch's face when he gave her the key to the safe deposit box, which was also the key to all his hopes and dreams. Greater love, Assia thought to herself, staring out of the window at the grey December sky.

The case was not over. Not yet.

THE OLD MAN WAS JUST ABOUT TO SETTLE DOWN FOR A LITTLE REST, WHEN ONE OF THE NURSES TAPPED LIGHTLY ON THE DOOR OF HIS ROOM.

"Just come to make you nice and comfortable," she announced cheerfully, entering with a pile of freshly laundered sheets.

Kirilovitch sighed. It was a strange phenomenon of hospital life that just as you were beginning to relax someone always came and disturbed you. Hospitals didn't run on the same logical rails as the outside world. Which was also why, the moment he'd dozed off last night, he'd been woken up and offered a sleeping pill.

The nurse donned thin rubber gloves. "Is your granddaughter coming to visit you today?" she asked chattily as she stripped off his top sheet, rolled it up and dropped it into a laundry bag.

"My...? Oh, yes, I think so," the old man lied, trying to preserve his dignity by turning over onto his side.

"Aww, that's nice, isn't it?" The nurse flapped one of the clean sheets over his body, then pulled it tight, tucking in the ends. "You need your family around you at Christmas, that's what I always say."

"Is it Christmas already?" he asked, struggling to free his arms from the straitjacket of his bed. Even after all this time away from his own country he still got confused about the date. In Russia, Christmas happened in January, not December.

"It's Christmas Eve, my love," the nurse informed him. She unhooked the clipboard hanging at the foot of his bed and ticked one of the boxes. Another task successfully completed.

Christmas. The birth of Christ. Kirilovitch tried unsuccessfully to remember the date of his own birthday. Ay! he thought despairingly. Things were bad when you couldn't remember something as basic as that. He could always look in his passport, of course. But which one? He had numerous passports. All with various identities, differing details. So how could he believe what was written there? It depended upon who he was at the time.

"Can I get you anything?" the nurse asked, as she peeled off her gloves and binned them. She picked up the old sheets and turned towards the door.

Ah. Now there's an interesting question, he thought. Silently, he concentrated upon all the things he wanted: to see his wife and daughter; an end to living in constant fear; some sort of viable future.

"A drink of water would be nice," he compromised.

The nurse refilled his glass with the tap water that tasted faintly of iron, made a jokey remark about him staying put and not running away. Then she bustled out. Places to go, patients to disturb. For a while the old man dozed peacefully. Then the door opened again. This time Assia entered the room, accompanied by Jazmin.

Kirilovitch awoke, levered himself awkwardly into a sitting position. He looked up at Assia. "So what's happening in the world?" he grunted.

Assia picked up a chair and placed it next to his bed. "We've found out how Nikolai tracked you down," she said. "The police have been checking the calls he made on his micro. It appears that there was a picture of the chess tournament in one of the London papers. Nikolai saw it, recognized you as one of the players, rang the organizers and got hold of the list of competitors. Then he used his contacts to work methodically through every name, visiting every address listed until he found you. And there's also the record of the calls he made to the people he hired to shoot you." Assia shook her head sadly. "I find it unbelievable that he managed to run rings around us for so long."

The old man gave her a thin smile. "Like I told you, Nikolai is a consummate strategist. Always several steps ahead of his opponent."

"Not any more," Assia said firmly. "The police have ample evidence from the calls, not to mention the attack on you. I don't think Nikolai Arkady will be stepping anywhere for a very long time."

"Hey, great news!" Jazmin added.

"And I've just spoken to the specialist," Assia continued. "He says they will discharge you soon after Christmas."

The old man bent his head in acknowledgement.

"Yeah, but that means you'll be stuck in hospital over the holiday!" Jazmin said. "It's so not fair."

Kirilovitch smiled at her. "I've got used to spending it on my own," he said gently. "It really doesn't matter."

"Mum?" Jazmin said, glancing expectantly across the bed.

Assia nodded at her. "I think maybe this year will be different," she said. "I've checked it out, and the staff will allow us to come in and celebrate here with you."

"We'll make sure you have a great time," Jazmin added. "Presents, crackers, Christmas dinner, the whole works."

"That sounds wonderful."

"If you're really lucky, I might even give you a game of chess in the afternoon – whoa, how good is that?"

The old man tried to look enthusiastic.

"And we'll make sure your cat doesn't miss out either," Assia went on. "I'm sure he'd appreciate a big turkey dinner, wouldn't he?"

Kirilovitch blinked away the moisture that had gathered at the corners of his eyes. "You're very kind," he muttered. "Thank you – thank you both."

There was a moment's silence.

Then he cut Assia a glance. "And afterwards?" he asked. "What happens then?"

It was the question Assia had been dreading. She took a deep breath, leaned across the bed and covered his hand with hers. "The Russian authorities are gradually rounding up everybody associated with Boris and Nikolai," she said. "Soon, you will be able to return to Russia, if that's what you want. Or you could go back to your flat in Paris and resume your old life, it's entirely up to you. Of course, we will help you in whatever way we can. It's the least we can do. As my boss told you, the ISA is very grateful to you for what you've done."

There was a long silence. The old man gave her a penetrating look, as if he was reading the unspoken message behind her words. All at once, a light seemed to go out at the back of his eyes. He sighed deeply and looked away. "I think I'd like to rest now," he said quietly.

Assia nodded. "I understand." She got up, and signalled to Jazmin that it was time to leave.

LATER, JAZMIN LAY IN BED LISTENING TO THE FAMILIAR NOISES OF THE FLAT WINDING DOWN FOR THE NIGHT: THE HEATING PIPES GURGLING GENTLY, THE SOUNDS OF A LATE-NIGHT CHAT SHOW ON the TV. She folded her arms behind her head and sighed contentedly. Tomorrow was Christmas Day, and even though she knew she was far too old and sophisticated to be excited at the prospect, she couldn't resist a small sliver of anticipation as she thought about the day ahead.

Earlier on, she had wrapped her presents and added them to the ones already under the brightly lit Christmas tree in the lounge. For her mum, she had bought a bottle of her favourite scent, some silver hoop earrings and a beautiful apricot-coloured angora jumper. There was the book on London for the old man (which she would take to the hospital later on tomorrow). She had even bought Zeb a present: a box of Belgian chocolates. Just in case he had got her something. And if he hadn't got her anything, she reasoned, she could always scoff them herself.

Jazmin's bedroom door creaked slowly open. There was the sound of something moving quietly across the room, then a small thump at the end of her bed. The cat had landed. It walked delicately up the bed towards her. Crouching down by her left shoulder, it began kneading the duvet rhythmically with its velvet paws, purring loudly. A joyous sound. Jazmin reached out a hand and stroked its soft head. "Hey, Happy Christmas, Cat," she murmured. Then she turned over onto her side and switched out the light.

It was a bitterly cold afternoon on the twenty-eighth of December. A man and a woman waited, muffled up against the icy wind, close together outside an old-style apartment block on a St. Petersburg street in the Liteyniy district. They double-checked the address, then swiftly and silently entered the building. Striding past the creaking lift, they climbed the bare concrete stairs until they reached the fifth floor. A long, dimly lit corridor, threadbarely carpeted, was fringed on either side by dark wooden doors. The air smelled of powerful disinfectant and stale cooking.

They walked down the corridor, came to a halt outside a door, and knocked.

The door was opened by a dark-haired young women in her early twenties.

The man stepped forward.

"*Dobry vocher,*" he said politely

"*Dobry vecher,*" the young woman responded automatically. She looked at them puzzled, frowning. She waited to see what they wanted.

"Natacha Kirilovitchova?" the man asked.

"*Da.*"

The man produced his wallet and extracted an official looking ID card. "Stash McGregor, ISA," he explained, handing her the card and tapping himself on the chest. He indicated the woman standing next to him: "Suki Smith, also ISA," he added.

A worried expression appeared upon the young woman's face. "*Ya ne ponamayu* – I don't understand," she said, shaking her head.

Now the woman stepped forward. She smiled reassuringly. "We've come about your father," she said in Russian.

"My father?" the girl looked bewildered. "My father is dead."

"Your father is not dead," Suki told her. "He's alive and well."

The girl's deep-blue eyes widened in shock and amazement. Then the colour drained out of her face. She staggered back, stuttered out a few broken words. Suki reached out and gently held her by the arm. "May we come in?" she asked gently. "We really need to talk to you and your mother.'

A WEEK LATER. AT SHEREMETEVO-2 AIRPORT, TWO WOMEN WERE STANDING BY THE ARRIVALS BOARD. THE OLDER OF THE TWO WAS AN ATTRACTIVE WOMAN IN HER LATE FIFTIES. HER DARK-BROWN hair, threaded with grey, was worn swept up with a silver clip into an elegant French pleat. The younger one, a beautiful girl in her early twenties, had brilliantly dark-blue eyes. Her rich burgundy-coloured hair was cut in a neat bob that framed her face and just touched her slender shoulders.

It was mid-afternoon. The sky outside the plate-glass windows was grey, the unwashed windows were also grey, as were the piles of dirty shovelled-up snow that lined the runways. The two women watched the board, which told them that the London plane had landed, and that passengers' baggage was now in the hall awaiting collection. They moved to the Arrivals area and waited, scanning the faces of the people as they came through the gate.

And eventually, an elderly grey-haired man carrying a navy travel bag and wearing a dark overcoat and a fur hat stomped through the barrier, then stood on the concourse, leaning on a stick and looking awkwardly around as if he had just landed on a strange planet.

The two women stared at him and exchanged unbelieving glances. For a moment, they hesitated. Then together they ran across the concourse, calling his name in broken voices, their arms outstretched, their eyes alight with love and welcome. The old man saw them, and the years suddenly seemed to fall away from him, as his face broke into a slow, unbelieving smile. Uttering a cry of joy, he dropped his stick and his travel bag and opened both his arms wide to enfold them.

The three people stood together on the busy forecourt, completely oblivious to the curious stares of the passers-by. They did not speak. There were no words to say at this moment in time. Words would come later. Much later. For now, they just stood and held each other tight, so tight it seemed to those around them as if they would never let each other go ever again.

JAZMIN REACHED FOR THE CARTON OF ORANGE JUICE AND POURED HERSELF A GLASS. "i HATE JANUARY," SHE GRUMBLED. "iT'S COLD AND iT'S WET AND NOTHiNG iNTERESTiNG EVER HAPPENS."

Assia shooed the black and white cat off the breakfast table. "That cat has learned how to open the fridge," she said crossly. "I came down this morning, and he was helping himself to leftovers."

Jazmin reached down and stroked the top of Tolstoy's soft head. "Aww, he's just an old softie," she said. The cat rubbed a furry cheek against her fingers and purred rustily.

"Hmmm." Assia pursed her lips. "An old softie who's hopefully going to join his real owner very soon."

Jazmin sipped her juice. "You know what?" she said. "I was thinking about Ivan Kirilovitch, and I just realized something."

"Oh yes?"

"He told me that in Russia they celebrate Christmas on the seventh of January," Jazmin said. She grinned. "So we *did* get him back with his family in time for Christmas, after all."

And she gave her mum a triumphant thumbs-up.

ABOUT THE AUTHOR

Carol Hedges is the successful author of several books for children and teenagers. Her writing has received much critical acclaim and her novel, *Jigsaw*, was shortlisted for the Angus Book Award and longlisted for the Carnegie Medal.

Carol has one grown-up daughter and lives in Hertfordshire with her husband, two cats and a lot of fish.

Don't miss Spy Girl's first mission
The Dark Side of Midnight

Jazmin Dawson is a super-cool secret agent with hi-tech kit and a hi-octane life of crime-busting...in her dreams! In reality, Jazmin is a schoolgirl with a serious snack habit, whose biggest battles are with her maths homework.

But then everything changes. Jazmin's mum, who *is* a spy, goes missing and Jazmin is sent to rescue her. Stepping off the plane in Prague, Jazmin finds herself at the centre of an international mystery, and with a dangerous mission to infiltrate a rogue scientific institute.

"This is an action-packed page-turner with a heart."
Books For Keeps

0 7460 6750 X

Coming in 2007...

Once Upon a Crime

Smart-talking, super-stylish spy girl Jazmin Dawson is back – to save the world from evil and total destruction. Well, not quite. In reality, she's a schoolgirl whose life is full of deadlines, doughnuts and discipline issues.

Jazmin's mum, Assia, has her own concerns. She's working on her most shocking case yet, the seemingly accidental death of a young freerunner. Soon Assia notices similarities between the boy's death and several other cases of apparent suicide – are the deaths all part of a sinister plot?

Nothing can prepare Assia for the terrifying truth, or the fact that Jazmin's life is in great danger...

9780746078334

For more **thrilling reads** check out
www.fiction.usborne.com

Rodman Philbrick

The Last Book in the Universe

"Nobody around here reads any more. Why bother, when you can just use a mindprobe needle and shoot all the images and excitement straight into your brain? I've heard of books, but they were long before I was born, in the backtimes before the Big Shake, when everything was supposedly perfect, and everybody lived rich.

In real life, nobody comes to your rescue. Believe me, I know. But then I met Ryter, this old gummy who had a lot of crazy ideas. Together we tried to change the world..."

Gritty, moving and provocative, *The Last Book in the Universe* is a vivid futuristic adventure from internationally acclaimed author, Rodman Philbrick.

"Philbrick has created some memorable characters in this fast-paced adventure, which will leave readers musing over humanity's future."   *Booklist*

0 7460 7439 5

Bernard Ashley

Smokescreen

Ellie hates leaving behind her friends, but the worst thing about moving to a pub by the canal is that the dark, swirling waters bring back traumatic memories. And Ellie's troubles only grow when she discovers the shady dealings that take place in the Regent's Arms on Friday nights.

There is somebody who could expose the truth – if only she could escape the evil gang that holds her captive.

Smokescreen is an electrifying thriller that twists and turns through the shadowy underworld of a dangerous trade.

0 7460 6791 7

Thom Madley

Marco's Pendulum

When Marco is dumped in Glastonbury for the summer with his weird hippy grandparents, he discovers the town is steeped in myth and legend. He thinks it's all rubbish, of course, until his granddad gives him a pendulum and teaches him the ancient art of dowsing. Then strange, disturbing things really start to happen...

Together with Rosa, another newcomer to Glastonbury, Marco discovers a terrible secret that's been buried for centuries. And as dark forces gather over the town, its evil looks set to be unleashed.

Mysterious, scary and utterly compelling, *Marco's Pendulum* is a powerful story about the magic found in real places.

0 7460 6760 7

Tim Wynne-Jones

The Boy in the Burning House

Jim doesn't want to believe that his missing father has been murdered but Ruth Rose is determined to help him root out the truth – no matter how painful or dangerous it is.

"This classy teenage thriller really gets the heart pumping... Phew – it's hot!"   *The Funday Times*

Shortlisted for the Guardian Children's Fiction Prize 2005
0 7460 6481 0

The Survival Game

When Burl runs away into the Canadian wilderness, he must find a way to survive and escape his bullying father's dangerous games for good.

"Just about everything you could possibly want from a book."   *Publishing News*

**Winner of the Canada Council Governor General's
Literary Award**
0 7460 6841 7